Claimed

THE SISTERS OF KILBRIDE

JAYNE CASTEL

WINTER MIST PRESS

Claimed, by Jayne Castel

Published by Winter Mist Press

ISBN: 978-0-473-54758-5 (paperback)

Edited by Tim Burton

Cover photography courtesy of www.shutterstock.com
Map by Jayne Castel
Celtic cross image courtesy of www.pixabay.com

Visit Jayne's website: www.jaynecastel.com

A widow intent on taking the veil. The guard who would lay down his life for her. The proposal that will alter their relationship forever. A powerful tale of unrequited love in Medieval Scotland.

Lady Drew MacKinnon doesn't belong anywhere. A widow who has never remarried, she decides that the time has come for her to do as society expects and take the veil. But as Drew is neither pious, nor obedient in nature, she knows her new path won't be an easy one.

Carr Broderick has served the MacKinnon clan loyally for years. And unbeknown to Drew, he's been in love with her for just as long. He offers to escort Drew to her new life at a priory on the Scottish mainland, but this last mission will cost him. He longs to tell her how he feels, yet she is a lady and he is a warrior without lands, riches, or title.

But when Lady Drew approaches Carr with a shocking proposal halfway through their journey, he might just have the chance he's always longed for. Or will he?

Historical Romances
by Jayne Castel

DARK AGES BRITAIN

The Kingdom of the East Angles series
Night Shadows (prequel novella)
Dark Under the Cover of Night (Book One)
Nightfall till Daybreak (Book Two)
The Deepening Night (Book Three)
The Kingdom of the East Angles: The Complete Series

The Kingdom of Mercia series
The Breaking Dawn (Book One)
Darkest before Dawn (Book Two)
Dawn of Wolves (Book Three)
The Kingdom of Mercia: The Complete Series

The Kingdom of Northumbria series
The Whispering Wind (Book One)
Wind Song (Book Two)
Lord of the North Wind (Book Three)
The Kingdom of Northumbria: The Complete Series

DARK AGES SCOTLAND

The Warrior Brothers of Skye series
Blood Feud (Book One)
Barbarian Slave (Book Two)
Battle Eagle (Book Three)
The Warrior Brothers of Skye: The Complete Series

The Pict Wars series
Warrior's Heart (Book One)
Warrior's Secret (Book Two)
Warrior's Wrath (Book Three)

The Pict Wars: The Complete Series

Novellas
Winter's Promise

MEDIEVAL SCOTLAND

The Brides of Skye series
The Beast's Bride (Book One)
The Outlaw's Bride (Book Two)
The Rogue's Bride (Book Three)
The Brides of Skye: The Complete Series

The Sisters of Kilbride series
Unforgotten (Book One)
Awoken (Book Two)
Fallen (Book Three)
Claimed (Epilogue novella)
The Sisters of Kilbride: The Complete Series

The Immortal Highland Centurions series
Maximus (Book One)
Cassian (Book Two)
Draco (Book Three)
The Laird's Return (Epilogue festive novella)
The Immortal Highland Centurions: The Complete Series

Stolen Highland Hearts series
Highlander Deceived (Book One)
Highlander Entangled (Book Two)
Highlander Forbidden (Book Three)
Highlander Pledged (Book Four)

Guardians of Alba series
Nessa's Seduction (Book One)
Fyfa's Sacrifice (Book Two)
Breanna's Surrender (Book Three)

Epic Fantasy Romances by Jayne Castel

***

To my wonderful readers ... this one is for you all!

***

Map

THE CLAN TERRITORIES
OF THE ISLE OF SKYE
IN THE 14TH CENTURY
THE MINCH
SOUND OF RAASAY
INNER SOUND
MAINLAND
MACLEOD
MACDONALD
MACKINNON
ISLE OF SKYE
ISLE OF RAASAY
SCALPAY
FRASER
MACDONALD OF SLEAT
SEA OF THE HEBRIDES

*It is never too late to be
what you might have been.*
—George Eliot

1

Bad Days

Dunan broch
MacKinnon Territory
Isle of Skye, Scotland

Winter, 1350 AD

SOME DAYS, IT was better to stay abed.

From the moment Lady Drew awoke in her frigid chamber to find that the hearth had gone out in the night, she resisted the urge to pull the blankets over her head and go back to sleep.

But retreating wasn't Drew's way—and so she gritted her teeth and climbed out of bed, wincing as her bare feet hit the ice-cold flagstones. She called for her maid—a sullen-faced lass named Cadha—thrice, before the young woman deigned to present herself. The lass's face was even sourer than usual when she finally appeared and helped Drew dress. She was so rough as she started to braid her mistress's hair that eventually Drew sent the lass scurrying away with a sharp reprimand.

Drew finished her hair herself—a task which took her an age, for her fingers were clumsy with cold.

By the time she joined her brother and his wife in the clan-chief's solar, they'd almost finished breaking their fast.

"We thought ye weren't joining us this morning, Drew," Craeg greeted her with a grin. He and Lady Coira sat together at the far end of the table. Her arrival had interrupted a passionate kiss.

"I slept in," Drew muttered, taking a seat at the table. She had the urge to complain about Cadha and yet held her tongue. Craeg was very good to her. She didn't want to appear ungrateful.

Instead, she reached for the last wedge of bannock. "I see ye left me plenty."

The tart edge to her voice made Craeg's grin widen. "Worry not, sister ... I'll have Kenzie bring up some more."

Sister.

Drew stilled for a heartbeat before dropping her gaze to the wedge of bannock she'd just placed on the dish before her.

By rights, Craeg shouldn't even want her here. Although he welcomed her continued presence in the broch, Drew felt like an interloper. She was part of the old guard, from a time when their elder brother had ruled this broch.

When Craeg had bested Duncan MacKinnon and his men in battle and ridden to Dunan to take his place, Drew had been too ill to care. But afterward, she'd braced herself for his hate, his vengeance.

There had been none.

Drew's mouth thinned as she started to butter her wedge of bannock. Craeg deserved a better family than the one he'd been born into.

For years, she'd known of his existence—the bastard Duncan had loathed. Their father had sired him off a local whore, and many years earlier, Duncan had run him out of Dunan, although not before he'd nearly beaten his younger brother to death. He'd thought never to hear from Craeg again, but instead, the Bastard had risen up against him as the leader of an outlaw band that had caused the MacKinnon clan-chief no end of trouble over the years.

Drew stifled a sigh and reached for the pot of heather honey. She was glad that Craeg now ruled the MacKinnon clan, but his presence here was also a painful reminder that she was powerless in this world. Although Drew was clever and capable, she'd never have been allowed to become clan-chief. She was a woman—and as such was destined to forever sit in a man's shadow.

Drew clenched her jaw, before her attention returned to the far end of the table. She shouldn't dwell on such things—she risked turning bitter.

Oblivious to her brooding, the clan-chief and his wife had forgotten that she was present.

Craeg gazed at Coira as he fed her a morsel of bannock, while she leaned toward him, her proud face soft with love. They made a beautiful pair, both dark-haired and tall. Craeg's moss-green eyes hooded then when Coira licked honey off his fingers. Her violet gaze darkened with sensual promise.

Drew's jaw tightened. *God's teeth, can't they keep their hands off each other when others are present?* She tore her gaze from the couple and glared down at her plate.

Every morning, she had to endure this. Usually, she just ignored them, but this morning, their behavior grated upon her. Once, it would have pleased her to see two people so in love; once, she'd have happily entered into the spirit and flirted with the nearest handsome man.

But these days, it just made her feel jaded.

Drew's chest tightened. Craeg and his love, Coira, certainly deserved the joy they'd found in each other. They'd passed through fire to reach this point—had braved war and plague—battling against the odds that had been stacked against them.

But here they were, seated in the clan-chief's solar, a pale winter sun filtering in through the open window while a fire roared in the hearth—healthy, content, and in love.

It was no good. Try as she might to deny it, Drew envied them.

She forced herself to take a bite of bannock and chewed it with grim determination. She'd been hungry when she'd taken a seat at the table, yet her appetite had vanished.

A dry crumb stuck in her throat then, and she coughed. Reaching for a cup of milk, she attempted to wash it down.

However, the crumb had irritated the back of her throat, and she suffered a coughing fit.

Eyes watering, Drew shifted her attention once more to her companions. Coira and Craeg were laughing over something one of them had just said. She may as well have been invisible. Would they have noticed if she'd choked to death in front of them?

With a huff, Drew pushed herself up from the table.

Aye, she should have stayed abed. This morning wasn't improving.

Drew strode from the solar and nearly collided with the man standing guard outside.

"Good morning, Lady Drew." Broad-shouldered and well-built with close-cropped blond hair, Carr Broderick stepped to one side to avoid Drew, his grey-blue gaze settling upon her. "Is something amiss?"

"No, Broderick," she snapped. "I just need to get outside and stretch my legs. I'm going mad cooped up in here."

Days of freezing, stormy weather had prevented her from taking her daily strolls, but in her present mood, she'd not be thwarted.

Drew strode along the hallway, heading back to her bed-chamber to fetch her fur cloak.

Broderick fell in step behind her.

Irritation surged, and Drew clenched her jaw. *Damn the man.* He followed her around like a hound. When Craeg had taken control of Dunan, Broderick had stepped down from his former role as Captain of the Dunan Guard to become her personal guard.

Wherever she went, there was Broderick a few paces back—her second shadow.

The urge to tell the man to go away rose within Drew, yet she swallowed it. The warrior was impervious to her sharp tongue. He'd made it clear months earlier that there were still plenty of folk—both within the broch, and in the village and lands surrounding it—who bitterly resented Duncan MacKinnon.

They saw her as his supporter, and according to Broderick, many folk still wished to have their revenge. Drew had scoffed at his concerns, yet she'd been unable to get him to cease shadowing her.

Doing her best to ignore her guard, she threw open the door to her bed-chamber and stalked inside.

Outdoors, the winter wind gusted across the bailey, tugging at Drew's cloak and slapping her exposed cheeks. She squinted up at the sky; it was filled with racing clouds, many of which were leaden and ominous.

"We shouldn't go far, Lady Drew," Broderick murmured behind her. "Rain is on its way."

"A few turns around the kirkyard won't hurt," she replied. Not waiting for his reply, she headed left, circuiting the base of the broch toward the South Gate. The guards there greeted her before allowing Drew and her guard to pass through into the windswept kirkyard beyond.

Drew entered the wide yard studded with mossy gravestones, just as thunder rumbled across the sky. Halting, she viewed the dark sky with a jaundiced eye.

"We should really go inside, milady," Broderick said, stopping at her side. "It's going to pelt down in a moment."

Drew cast him a sharp look. "Ye go back if a little rain bothers ye, Broderick," she snapped. "But I'm going for a walk."

With that, she picked up her skirts and strode down the path.

Drew had just turned off the gravel, intent on weaving her way through the gravestones, when she stepped upon something slippery.

There wasn't even time to cry out in alarm. Her feet flew out from under her, and she fell, arms cartwheeling—straight into Carr Broderick's waiting embrace.

It was like hitting a wall. Drew's breath gusted out of her as his brawny arms fastened about her torso. A heartbeat later, he set her upon her feet.

Shaken, Drew looked down to see that she'd stepped into an enormous cowpat.

Broderick snorted. "Looks like someone's *coos* have gotten free again."

Drew's mouth twisted, and she hiked up her skirts, peering down at her leather boots that were now covered in dung. "These were new," she muttered.

"A bit of soap and water will see them right again, milady," he replied.

Drew glanced up sharply, her gaze meeting his. Was she imagining it, or was that amusement she saw there? His mouth was turning up at the corners.

"Laugh and I shall slap ye," she warned, her gaze narrowing. His mouth quirked into a rare smile at her threat, incensing her. "I'm warning ye, Broderick."

At that moment, thunder clapped directly overhead, so loudly that Drew cringed against Broderick's broad chest.

They both waited, breaths indrawn, and then cold rain started to patter down.

Boom. Thunder crashed again, and a sheet of lightning illuminated the western sky.

And then, as if God had just upturned a bucket of icy water, rain poured down from the heavens, drenching them both.

There hadn't even been time for Drew to pull up her hood. Not that it mattered—for the rain was so heavy it would have soaked the fur in instants.

Water ran down Drew's face, blinding her. Wiping it out of her eyes, she pulled back from Broderick and met his gaze once more. "Don't say a word," she growled.

Back in her bed-chamber, Drew removed her sodden cloak and hung it up next to the hearth. Cadha had relit the fire while her mistress had been out, and now a large lump of peat burned.

She'd done her best to clean her boots downstairs but had eventually left them for the servants to deal with.

Drew stretched her chilled fingers out before the fire, sighing as the heat soaked through her flesh. As much as she hated to admit it, Broderick had been right. She should have taken notice of those dark clouds before going out for a walk. However, she'd never confess such to him. The rain now lashed against the closed shutters of the bed-chamber's single small window, thunder booming so loudly that the broch's stone walls shook from the force of the storm.

Listening to it, Drew's eyes flickered closed. Today was a sign. Finally, after months of wavering, she had to take action. Dunan didn't feel like her home any longer—it hadn't in a while. She felt utterly superfluous here.

Alone in her chamber, she made the decision she'd put off for too long.

With another sigh, Drew opened her eyes and moved away from the hearth, before taking a seat at the nearby desk. A single stubby candle flickered there, casting a soft light across a neatly stacked pile of parchment, the wax tablets she used for sealing letters, and her inkpot and quill.

Lighting another candle, Drew helped herself to a leaf of parchment. However, before she reached for her quill, she hesitated. She'd delayed this moment deliberately. To write this letter felt so *final*. Once she sent it off, her days at Dunan would be numbered, for she doubted the request she was about to make would be refused.

That's the point, isn't it?

Jaw firming in resolution, she dipped the quill into the inkwell and began to write.

2

Welcome News

"LADY DREW ... A message has arrived for ye."

Drew glanced up from her bowl of porridge to see that Carr Broderick had joined them in the solar. Cheeks ruddy with cold, his grey-blue eyes serious with purpose, he held out a roll of parchment.

Taking the scroll with a nod, Drew's pulse quickened. She received few missives these days—and as nearly three weeks had passed since she'd sent her letter away, she knew that this was the reply she'd been awaiting.

Broderick cast her a questioning look, before he stepped back, to take up his position near the door. She saw from his expression that he'd sensed her nervousness, and the realization made her tense.

I've been spending too much time in his company, she thought, breaking the wax seal on the scroll. *The man reads me too well these days.*

She and Broderick had lived under the same roof for many years, but before Duncan's downfall, they'd had little contact. The warrior—who'd come to foster at Dunan as a lad and then remained to serve her brother—was still largely an enigma to Drew. She wondered how he felt about his demotion from Captain to lowly guard.

Surely it must gall him to spend his days at her beck and call?

It was a considerable drop in rank, yet if Broderick minded, he never let it show.

Glancing away from her guard, Drew unfurled the parchment and scanned the missive within. It was brief, just a few lines, but as she read them, Drew's breathing slowed.

"What is it, Drew?" At the end of the table, Craeg put down the wedge of bannock he'd been about to take a bite from, his handsome face tightening.

Not for the first time, Drew marveled at just how much he looked like their dead brother. The same wavy peat-dark hair, arrogant bearing, and chiseled jaw. Yet unlike Duncan, who'd had iron-grey eyes like Drew—a legacy from their mother—Craeg's eyes were a warm moss-green. He also bore a long, thin scar that stretched down from temple to cheek, narrowly missing his left eye. Duncan had given him that.

His mother must have been a kind woman, for a great sense of humanity tempered the MacKinnon arrogance in Craeg.

No wonder the folk of this land love him.

"It's a message from my mother," Drew replied, lowering the parchment.

"Ill tidings?" Coira asked softly.

Drew shook her head and forced a smile. "No, actually ... welcome news. She has spoken to the Prioress of Inishail Priory in Argyll ... as I've asked. And they will admit me as a novice."

Craeg's gaze drew wide. "Ye are taking the veil?"

The incredulity in his voice made Drew stiffen. It didn't surprise her that found the idea preposterous; most folk who knew her well would.

Lady Drew MacKinnon wasn't the sort of woman one would expect to find in a convent.

"Aye," she replied calmly.

"But why?" Coira asked. Meeting the woman's eye, Drew saw the consternation there. Of course, Coira knew what it was to live as a nun—for she'd resided at Kilbride

Abbey for a decade—before war and pestilence uprooted her life forever.

Drew inhaled slowly. She was aware then that Craeg and Coira weren't the only people present staring at her—she could feel Carr Broderick's gaze boring into her too. Glancing his way, she saw that he wore a stunned expression as if she'd just slapped him.

Drew's lips parted. She was about to offer some lie about how much she missed her mother and how the woman had begged her to come join her at Inishail. The words rose within her, but then they choked in her throat.

She cared for these people—the realization jolted through her—and they deserved honesty.

"I never expected to be welcome here after Duncan's demise," she said finally. "I thought that ye would cast me out for being his sister."

"But ye are *my* sister too," Craeg reminded her, frowning. "And I am glad of it."

Drew's throat thickened as she shook her head. Craeg's kindness made this harder than she'd expected. "Dunan is *yer* home now," she said, her throat aching, "but I no longer belong in this broch ... I haven't for a while. The truth is that I feel useless here."

"Of course ye belong here." Craeg's frown deepened. "Dunan was yers long before it was mine."

"Aye, once. But every chamber, every corner, is a reminder of the past," Drew replied. It was true. She had grown up within these walls, the daughter of a callous father and shrewish mother—and then had lived under her cruel elder brother's rule for far too long. Duncan MacKinnon's presence still lingered here, a stain on her conscience.

She had to make a new start elsewhere. As a nun, she could do some good perhaps. Here in Dunan, she felt like an encumbrance, even if Craeg and Coira would never admit as much.

"The last few months have changed me," Drew admitted with a half-smile. "I feel a stranger within these walls."

"Give it time," Craeg said after a pause. Her brother was no longer frowning; he just looked worried. "It might just be the winter's gloom getting to ye ... ye'll feel different once the weather warms."

Next to him, Coira watched Drew, a thoughtful expression upon her face. She'd said little since her sister-by-marriage's news, yet Drew knew that Coira understood how she felt.

Sometimes folk just didn't fit into their old life anymore.

"Time won't change how I feel ... or my decision," Drew answered, stubbornness setting in. "The decision has been made. Space has been made for me at Inishail, and I will leave as soon as I'm able."

Coira's gaze widened. "So soon ... can't ye wait till the spring thaw at least?"

Drew shook her head. "I'm not fond of farewells ... I'd rather not prolong this one."

Silence fell in the solar. It was another chill morning, and a fire roared in the hearth as the wind whistled against the walls of the broch.

"I will organize an escort for ye," Craeg said finally, his voice heavy, his gaze shuttered. "I can't have ye traveling to Argyll alone."

"I will lead it, if I may." A low voice interrupted.

Drew's attention shifted to Broderick. The surprise she'd glimpsed upon his face had gone, and now he wore a somber expression as if they were organizing a burial.

"Thank ye, Broderick," Craeg replied with a nod before Drew had the chance to speak up. "Gather a party of six warriors. My sister must be well-guarded on her journey."

"Are ye sure ye have thought this through?"

Drew had been awaiting Coira's question. The silence
in the women's solar had grown deafening as the
morning stretched on. The pair of them sat near the
hearth. Drew was embroidering the hem of a summer
kirtle, while Coira wound wool onto a spindle.

Glancing up, Drew saw that her sister-by-marriage
was frowning, her fine dark brows knitted together.

"Aye, I have," Drew replied. "Why? Do ye question my
choice?"

"Taking the veil isn't a decision to be taken lightly,"
Coira replied, her voice low and firm. "It's not an easy
life for many. I've known women who've regretted it."

Drew shrugged. "Ye enjoyed the life of a nun well
enough, didn't ye?"

Coira sighed and lowered the spindle to her lap. "Aye
... although for me it was an escape. At Kilbride, I was
free of male attention, free from brutality."

The words hung between them, and Drew tensed. Her
initial reaction to Coira's concerns had been flippant, yet
she couldn't continue to act that way now. Not when she
knew that the brutality Coira spoke of had been suffered
at the hands of Duncan MacKinnon.

Drew had so much to thank Coira for. Months earlier,
she'd appeared at Drew's bedside like an angel of mercy
at her darkest hour. She'd brought her back from the
edge. In the moons that had passed since Drew had
recovered from the sickness, Coira had treated her like a
sister.

"I remember ye telling me that ye weren't pious
before going to Kilbride," Drew said after a pause. "Yer
life at the abbey gave ye purpose. I want to find such
meaning for my own life."

Coira held her gaze, her expression shadowed. "Ye
don't need to take the veil to find purpose."

Drew frowned, her irritation rising. "Ye think I'm ill-
suited, don't ye?"

Coira's mouth quirked. "Aye. Ye are strong-willed to a
fault. I hope the prioress knows what she's in for."

"Well then," Drew sniffed. "Perhaps Inishail will be
good for me."

A heavy silence fell between them. When Coira broke it, her gaze was probing. "All those times I've asked ye to join me in prayer at the kirk, and ye refused. Ye can understand why I'm surprised by yer decision to become a nun. It seems so ... out of character."

Drew stuck her needle into her embroidery and leaned back in her chair. Of course Coira found her behavior odd; her sister-by-marriage deserved an explanation she supposed. "Dunan kirk holds ill memories for me," Drew admitted after a pause. "When I was a lass, Ma used to make me kneel for hours there before the altar after I'd misbehaved. I grew to hate the place. And these days, whenever I enter the kirk, all I can see is Father Athol crumpled before the altar after Duncan stabbed him."

Coira's violet eyes shadowed at these words, and when she replied, she deliberately avoided speaking of the man who'd driven her to take the veil many years earlier. "Do ye really want to live under the same roof as yer mother again?" she asked.

A sigh escaped Drew. She hadn't missed Lorna MacKinnon in the time since she'd departed Dunan, yet she decided against admitting that to Coira. She wasn't going to Inishail for her mother's sake anyway, but for her own. "Folk can change," she said crisply, picking up her embroidery once more. "Perhaps all the years at Inishail have softened her."

3

I'll Never Know Now

THEY RODE OUT of Dunan on a grey, wet dawn, headed southeast toward the coastal village of Kyleakin. The journey would take them the better part of the day, and so Broderick had insisted upon an early start.

The good-byes were awkward, difficult, as Drew knew they would be.

Craeg and Coira came out into the bailey to see her off. Their faces were pale with sleep and drawn from the chill damp that rose off the slick cobblestones. Wrapped in fur cloaks, the couple watched Drew lead her palfrey from the stables before Craeg stepped forward and approached her.

"There's still time to change yer mind," he murmured. "No one will think less of ye for it, Drew."

Throat constricting, Drew shook her head. She should have known her brother would make this hard for her.

My brother.

Aye, although she'd never set eyes on the man before last summer, Craeg MacKinnon was the brother she'd always wanted, the brother she'd wished Duncan could have been. He was younger than her by nearly three winters, her baby brother, yet he towered over her now as he reached out and took her hands with his.

Her fingers were chilled already, yet his hands were warm and dry. Why was it that men always had such warm hands? Winters were a trial for Drew, for she spent months with numb fingers and toes, and chilblains that rose in red, itchy welts on her hands and feet.

"I know ye wouldn't, Craeg," she said softly. "But the fact remains that I'd leave sooner or later … it would only prolong the inevitable."

"Please send word when ye reach Inishail," Coira said, stepping up to her husband's side. "It's not safe for travelers these days."

Drew tensed. She'd heard that in the wake of the sickness that had swept over Scotland, there had been a rise in lawlessness upon the mainland. Merchants had brought word that brigands patrolled many highways and preyed upon travelers.

Forcing a smile, Drew met Coira's warm gaze. "Aye … but I should be safe enough with Broderick and yer men as my escort." She glanced back at Craeg. "Are ye sure ye can spare them?"

"Of course I can," he replied with a snort. "Coira's right. Let us know ye have arrived safely at the priory." Craeg shifted his gaze over Drew's shoulder then, at where Carr Broderick had just led his horse out into the yard. Drew noted how the men's gazes fused for a long moment. They had an odd relationship, Craeg and Broderick. Craeg had allowed the guard to remain on in Dunan and was cordial with him, yet there was a reserve between the two men. The shadow of Broderick's past allegiances hung over them.

He's not that different to me, Drew thought, casting a glance over her shoulder to see that her guard was holding Craeg's eye. *He doesn't belong here either.* What would happen to him once he delivered her to Inishail Priory?

"Look after her, Broderick," Craeg rumbled.

The guard nodded curtly. "With my life, MacKinnon."

Pushing back her hood, Drew peered up at the sky, hoping to see the pale glimmer of the sun. However, the clouds had sunk low, obscuring the soaring mountains that etched the sky to the west and the south. A misty rain continued to fall, although fortunately, there was no wind this morning.

It was going to be a wet ride to Kyleakin.

Drew inhaled slowly, drawing the fresh, damp air into her lungs. It was a relief to be away from Dunan. Her vision had blurred dangerously when Craeg had pulled her into a fierce hug and then Coira had done the same.

She'd stumbled, half-blind, over to where her grey palfrey sat patiently awaiting her and had allowed Broderick to boost her up side-saddle. It had taken all her will not to dig her heel into her mount's flank and send it careening out of the bailey.

Emotional displays weren't something that Drew favored. She hated the sensation of losing control.

Clattering out of Dunan's North Gate a short while later, she'd actually scrubbed away a tear that had treacherously escaped. However, her dignity was intact, even if her chest felt as if a boulder sat upon it.

Fortunately, the farther they traveled from Dunan, the more the pressure upon her chest lightened. Drew realized that whatever the outcome, she'd made the right decision to leave. The past, and all its memories, was behind her now.

A new start lay in Argyll. She wasn't going to pretend that adjusting to a life of prayer and solitude would be easy, but it would be a refreshing change from an existence that had been stifling her for a long while now.

Drew rode near the head of the column, just behind Carr Broderick and one other, while the remaining guards traveled behind her. They rode in companionable silence, something Drew was grateful for; not that Broderick was ever one to indulge in idle chatter.

Her gaze rested upon him now.

Like her, Broderick had pushed back his hood, letting the misty rain fall upon his head. Unlike many men, who grew their hair long, he wore his pale blond hair short. The rain had darkened it, and as she watched, he raked a hand through his hair, leaving it in spiky disarray.

The cloak highlighted the breadth of his shoulders, the strength of his muscular body. How old was Broderick? Around thirty winters perhaps—five or six years younger than her. A man in his prime, a warrior, who'd given his loyalty to the wrong man and was now paying for it.

He'd been a constant overbearing presence over the past months, yet a part of her was glad he'd offered to lead her escort.

Carr Broderick made her feel safe, protected.

Strangely, few other men—besides her half-brother—had made her feel that way. In truth, she struggled to understand males at all. Most of them seemed rough-mannered and limited in understanding compared to women. Perhaps that was why she'd remained a widow after Egan's passing.

Her husband had been over twenty-five years her elder, but that wouldn't have mattered if she'd desired him. Even now, she suppressed a shudder when she remembered being bedded by him. Egan had been a tall, thin man with watery pale blue eyes and a weak chin. An insipid, perfunctory lover, he was the sort to climb on, do the deed, and then roll off and go to sleep.

She might have overlooked the fact he was a disappointing lover if they'd been friends, yet Egan had little time for her. He was a 'man's man', who preferred to be out hawking or in the Great Hall drinking with the other warriors.

It had been shocking, the day he'd died, choking on a trout bone, but she hadn't grieved for him.

They'd been wed for years, although her womb had never quickened. A bairn might have given her a focus, might have made him warmer toward her. A decade of marriage, and she felt like she hardly knew him.

Drew's mouth compressed at her husband's memory, and she focused her attention on her palfrey's pricked ears.

She tried not to dwell on the past much these days. But seeing Craeg and Coira so obviously happy together, so in love, had just highlighted the emptiness of her own marriage. The attraction between them crackled in the air, like the heavy sultry atmosphere before a summer squall.

What was it like to feel like that?

Drew gnawed at her lower lip and urged her mount into a brisk trot as the company crested a hill.

I'll never know now.

She'd once had dreams. After Egan died, she'd looked around for a suitable husband, for a man she desired. She thought she'd found it in Gavin MacNichol. The MacNichol clan-chief was only a few years her elder. Blond and blue-eyed, with a boyish smile, and a tall, muscular build that drew a woman's eye, Gavin, unfortunately, hadn't been interested in her at all. A widower, Gavin had eventually remarried, to his dead wife's sister, but he'd never once encouraged Drew's affections.

Drew's cheeks warmed then as she remembered how she'd thrown herself at him on more than one occasion. The last time, she'd let herself into his bed-chamber during a visit to Dunan—and he'd rebuffed her.

I deserved that.

Aye, she had—but that hadn't taken the sting out of it. She was much warier around men these days. And soon, once she reached Inishail Priory, she wouldn't have to deal with them at all.

Carr slowed his horse so that he rode shoulder to shoulder with Lady Drew's palfrey. The weather had worsened as the day progressed, the veil of rain closing in around them.

"How are ye faring, milady?" he asked. "Do ye need to rest?"

Drew shook her head, her pert features set in a dogged look he knew well. "We rested at noon," she pointed out. "I'd prefer to press on for Kyleakin ... how much farther is it?"

"Not much ... the rain has slowed us, but we should reach the port before dusk."

She inclined her head, fixing him with that mesmerizing iron-grey gaze of hers. "Will we be able to find passage tomorrow?"

He nodded, taking in the loveliness of her face. She had an impish quality to her beauty, which gave her a youthful air. Her hair, coiled in its tight braids, clung to her scalp, while the mist coated her creamy skin. "There's a boat at dawn bound for Kyle of Lochalsh ... if the weather doesn't take a turn for the worse, we shall be taking that."

Sometimes it was difficult for Carr to concentrate when talking to Drew. He'd made a point of riding ahead, of keeping his gaze upon the highway before them and scanning the roadside for any sign of danger. However, when they'd stopped at noon, his attention kept returning to her.

Now he knew that their time together was coming to an end, his gaze wanted to feast upon this woman, to memorize every line upon her face.

But even as he gazed at her, his heart felt as if it were slowly shrinking. Lady Drew was leaving, shutting herself forever in a priory—a place where he'd never set eyes on her again. A familiar heaviness pressed down upon him at the thought. Never again would he hear the velvet timbre of her voice, the music of her laughter. Never again would he inhale the scent of lily as she walked by, or meet that knowing iron-grey gaze. Ever since she'd announced her news, a dark shadow had settled over his world.

Holding his gaze, Drew's mouth pursed. "What is it, Broderick?" She reached up and touched her cheek. "Do I have mud on my face?"

Satan's cods, he was staring.

This was his chance. He could tell her how he felt, could lay himself bare before her and beg her not to take the veil. Yet the words wouldn't come—they never had.

Carr shook his head and ripped his gaze from hers. "No, milady," he mumbled.

An instant later, he urged his horse forward, leaving Drew to ride by herself once more.

4

Taking Supper Together

DREW WAS SHIVERING when they reached their destination at last—*The King's Arms* in Kyleakin. The port village, a cluster of white-washed cottages huddled against a brown hillside studded with dark pines, sat facing a grey expanse of water. The mainland lay to the north, just in front of Kyleakin, but this afternoon, a bank of dense cloud obscured it.

In the stables behind the inn, the company dismounted their tired horses.

"I'll see to yer palfrey, milady," Broderick said brusquely, addressing her for the first time since their awkward exchange earlier that afternoon. "Ye had best get indoors before ye catch cold."

Teeth chattering, Drew obliged. Her fur mantle dragged down at her as she crossed the straw-strewn yard and entered the inn through a narrow doorway. Warmth embraced her when she stepped inside, as did an array of smells: the fug of peat-smoke, the greasy odor of roasting mutton, the scent of sawdust, and the hoppy tang of freshly brewed ale.

Drew sighed and paused for a moment, taking in the crowded common room before her.

She hadn't been inside an inn or tavern for years now, not since before she'd wed. She'd forgotten how cozy they were, especially when the weather outdoors was so gloomy.

A huge hearth roared at one end of the room, and low beams crisscrossed the space. A number of oaken tables dotted the floor, although Drew's gaze went to the comfortable-looking booths that lined the walls.

She was aware then of the patrons—most of them men—turning their heads to look at the newcomer. Curiosity flowered on their faces, although Drew ignored them. Instead, her gaze went to the portly young man who hurried toward her.

"Lady Drew MacKinnon?" he asked, breathless, his eyes bright.

Drew nodded, glad that Broderick had sent word ahead of their arrival the day before. He'd wanted to make sure the inn could accommodate them all.

"Did ye have a good journey from Dunan, milady?"

"It was wet and cold," Drew answered honestly. She was aware then that everyone in the common room was now gawking at her. The innkeeper's excited greeting hadn't escaped any of them. "I'm looking forward to a hot bath and a meal."

"And I will ensure ye receive both, milady," the innkeeper assured her. "Come ... I shall escort ye to yer chamber. I will have hot water brought up for ye immediately." He ushered her across the crowded floor toward the wooden stairs that led to the upper level of the inn, his manner suddenly nervous. At first Drew wondered at his urgency, and then, when she felt intent male gazes follow her to the stairs, her spine stiffened.

Suddenly, she wished that Broderick had accompanied her in here. She remembered his warnings about the ill-will many folk still bore her dead brother.

She hoped no one inside *The King's Arms* had a score to settle with Duncan MacKinnon.

With a sigh, Drew sank down into the hot water. Her eyes fluttered shut, and she inhaled deeply. Lavender and rosemary—the innkeeper's wife had added a special oil to the water, one which created a scent that now floated like a cloud above the steaming bath.

Lord, this feels good.

The day's journey had chilled Drew to the marrow. Her hands and feet had felt like lumps of ice as she entered her bed-chamber. When she'd peeled off her clothing, she noted that even her léine, the long ankle-length tunic she wore under her kirtle, was wet.

Broderick was right—she risked catching a chill.

However, the hot, scented water was a balm, and as she lay there, she could literally feel the heat seeping through her chilled limbs and restoring them once more.

Eventually, Drew opened her eyes and took in her surroundings. Although much smaller than her bed-chamber back in Dunan, the room was very pleasant. White-washed with dark wooden beams overhead, it had a tiny shuttered window and a large bed with soft cushions filled with goose-down. Deerskins covered the wooden floors, and a hearth burned in one corner.

This chamber made the one she'd left behind seem cold and austere in comparison.

Don't get too used to it, she reminded herself. *Soon ye shall be sleeping in a nun's cell.*

It was a sobering reminder. A nun's life would be very different to the one she'd known until now. She had to prepare herself for the lack of comfort.

Drew's belly tightened as she allowed herself to think ahead, to imagine how she'd soon spend her days. There wasn't any point in shying away from it. Drew had always prided herself on being a realist. Entering the priory would be far less of a shock if she mentally prepared herself first.

During their last morning in the women's solar together, Coira had spelled out the realities of a nun's life for her. No longer would she have a large, soft bed; no longer would she wear brightly-colored kirtles. The rich meals at Dunan would be nothing more than a pleasant memory. She would likely have to cut her hair off and would wear a black habit for the rest of her life. She would also have to pray several times a day.

The heaviness in her stomach increased. Perhaps imagining the life before her wasn't a wise idea after all.

Drew sank further into the steaming water.

Glancing down, she let her gaze travel over her naked body. She'd regained flesh again after being sick last summer. Even so, the illness that had nearly claimed her life had left its mark upon her; pink scars remained from the boils that Coira had lanced. They were fading, but in the hot water still looked evident.

Drew suppressed a shudder. She'd been so weak after that sickness, so thin, that she couldn't sit down without putting a soft cushion under her backside.

She wasn't bony these days though. Her body had a pleasant softness to it; not that its appearance mattered much. Apart from Egan, no man had ever looked upon her nakedness.

And now no one would. Once she took the veil, men wouldn't see her as a woman any longer.

Just as well, for life in the priory will turn me into a stringy fowl, Drew thought ruefully. Coira had also told her how physically demanding the life of a nun was.

Drew sighed. Her thoughts were going around in circles and ruining her enjoyment of the bath. If this was her last soak in a tub, with scented oils and the sound of the rain pattering against the wooden shutters, then she wanted it to be a pleasant memory.

With that, Drew slid down, and, holding her breath, sank completely under the water, letting the liquid heat chase all thought away.

She bathed until the water cooled. Then, reluctantly, Drew climbed out and dried herself off as she listened to the storm rattle the shutters. She was glad to be indoors on a night such as this.

She was seated on the edge of the bed, clad in just a léine, teasing out the knots in her long dark hair with a wooden comb, when a soft knock sounded on the door.

"Lady Drew ... it's Broderick."

Drew paused in combing her hair. "Aye ... what is it?"

"The innkeeper wants to know if ye'd like any supper?"

Drew's belly growled in response. She had eaten a quick meal of bread and cheese at noon and didn't intend to miss supper. "Of course," she called back.

"Very well, milady ... I shall bring it up now."

Drew was about to thank him when she hesitated. She could dine here alone, but the common room had looked so warm and inviting. Soon, all her meals would take place in a grim priory refectory.

"Wait," she replied, casting aside her comb and rising to her feet. "Give me a few moments, and I shall join ye downstairs."

Carr took a draft of ale, savoring the sharp, hoppy taste on his tongue. *The King's Arms* in Kyleakin was known throughout the isle for its fine drink.

Sighing, Carr leaned back against the upholstered back of the booth he'd taken. The innkeeper had cleared a booth near the hearth as well as two tables on the floor for Carr's men. However, Carr had noted a tension in the air when he stepped into the common room. Unsurprisingly, most of the patrons in here were male—save two women, merchants' wives most likely, who were enjoying supper with their husbands across the room.

Carr's gaze traveled around the smoky space, noting the cool glances he and his men were receiving. Of course, they all wore sashes of MacKinnon plaid: pine green crisscrossed with red.

Kyleakin was a crossroads, a port that sat on the borders of two lands—MacKinnon and MacDonald—but a village that allied itself with neither clan. As such, it attracted those who didn't belong anywhere.

The King's Arms was a good establishment and served excellent ale, yet Carr knew it was wise not to let his guard down here.

He'd just finished observing a group of men playing knucklebones at a table a few yards away—noting that they seemed to be showing more attention to him and his men than to their game—when a flash of emerald green on the stairs across the room caught his eye.

As promised, Lady Drew had joined them.

Carr wasn't sure how he felt about her decision to take supper downstairs. It wasn't something a 'lady' did. And yet, Drew was soon to leave her old life behind her, so what did it matter?

On a purely selfish level, it would mean he got to share a meal with her—something he rarely did. The only time he'd sat at the same table as her to eat was that morning he'd discovered she was ill with the plague. Dunan had been largely deserted that day, as most of its inhabitants were either dead, sick, or had fled. He'd brought up a tray of bannocks to her solar before realizing that she had a fever.

Clad in a becoming green kirtle, her peat-brown hair twisted into a soft knot upon her head, Drew glided across the sawdust-strewn floor like a queen.

Carr's gaze tracked her as she walked—and so did every man in the place. Drew ignored them all. She'd grown up in a broch of rowdy men; she was used to being stared at and knew just how to quell a lecherous look with an icy glance.

"Good eve, Broderick," she slid into the booth and favored him with a smile that made Carr's pulse accelerate. "What's for supper?"

"Roast mutton, braised onions, and bread," he replied, pushing a full tankard of ale across to her. "Apologies … it won't be the fare ye are used to."

Drew huffed a laugh. "It'll be better than what awaits me in Inishail … Coira's filled me in on what to expect. I hear nuns exist on coarse bread, over-cooked vegetables, and gruel."

5

A Confession to Make

CARR BRODERICK SMILED, and Drew stilled a moment. The man hardly ever let his mouth curve in mirth. He usually wore an austere expression, his gaze watchful and guarded.

But seated in the booth, his hand curled around a tankard of ale, he looked the most at ease Drew had ever seen him.

The smile erased years from his face. He was younger than her, yet she often forgot that, for severity had carved lines into his forehead and caused grooves to bracket his mouth.

And yet when he smiled, she noticed that he had handsome features and a sensual mouth.

"I'm sure the food won't be that bad at Inishail," he said, still smiling.

The arrival of the innkeeper at their table with plates of food forestalled Drew's response. The rich aroma of roast mutton and braised onions wafted across the table, and Drew's mouth filled with saliva.

"I hope ye are right, Broderick," she said once the innkeeper had departed with the assurance that he was at her disposition if she needed the slightest thing. "But

I've gotten quite spoiled over the years. I fear the abbess might find me a bit haughty."

"Haughty, aye," he replied, his mouth quirking. "However, I wouldn't call ye spoiled, milady. When toil is necessary, ye have never turned yer back on it. Folk will remember how ye regularly brought baskets of food to them so they didn't starve over the winter."

Drew sucked in a surprised breath. That had to be the longest discourse she'd ever heard from her taciturn guard. His frankness unbalanced her. The urge to gently chide him for his words rose within Drew, yet she prevented herself.

They were away from Dunan, and the new setting had loosened both their tongues. She liked seeing this new side to Broderick. If she mocked him, he'd just retreat into his shell and they'd pass their meal in tense silence.

"Will they?" she murmured after a pause. "I fear many of them can't see past the fact that I am Duncan MacKinnon's sister. They still look for someone to blame … and tar me with the same brush."

"And yet they saw ye welcome Craeg as clan-chief. A loyal sister wouldn't have done so."

Drew snorted. "They probably judge me for that too," she replied, reaching for the half-loaf of bread the innkeeper had given her and ripping off a chunk. "Not everyone has such a rosy view of me, as ye well know." Drew paused there, suddenly aware of how bitter she sounded. "But ye are right. I did welcome Craeg. The MacKinnons needed a clan-chief. Bastard or not, he was heir."

"Ye were relieved … we all were," Carr replied, his gaze never wavering from hers. "Ye didn't want Duncan to return."

The half-smile Drew had been wearing slipped. "Ye are right, I didn't." She motioned to the untouched plate of food before him. "Go on … dig in, before it gets cold."

They started on their meals. It was simple yet delicious fare. The mutton had been slow-roasted—for most of the day, it seemed—as it fell apart in tender chunks. The onions were sweet, and the bread tasty and fresh. Washed down with the cool ale, it was the perfect meal.

Drew savored every mouthful, and she noted that Broderick did the same.

Around them, the rumble of conversation rose and fell in the common room. The noise grew increasingly raucous as the inn's patrons consumed tankard after tankard of ale. A harpist had set himself up upon a stool to one side of the fire. The lad was playing a jaunty tune, yet the melody was lost in the roar of surrounding voices.

Eventually, as her belly started to signal that it was full, Drew leaned back in her seat and observed her supper companion. Broderick was wiping up the gravy off his plate with the last of his bread. Like most men, he had an impressive appetite.

It was pleasant sitting here, lulled by the warmth of the fire and good food and ale. If she could freeze a moment in time from the past years, it would be this one.

"I planned to turn against Duncan, ye know?" she said finally, breaking the companionable silence between them. "I even asked Ross Campbell if he'd stand with me."

Broderick's eyes widened at this admission. "Ye did?"

Drew nodded. It was a treacherous thing she was revealing, yet what did it matter? Craeg was the MacKinnon clan-chief now. "It was just before Campbell ran away with Leanna ... so it wasn't much help to me." She observed his facial expression before she continued. "That's not the only betrayal against Duncan I committed ... later, when Campbell freed Leanna from my brother's bed-chamber, I helped them get out of the broch."

Broderick let out a slow exhale and leaned back. "That was a risk indeed, milady. If he'd ever found out, things would have gone ill for ye."

"I know ... but my conscience was bothering me." Her mouth curved at the arch look he now favored her with. "Aye ... maybe I'm not as cold-hearted as everyone believes."

He smiled. His right cheek dimpled slightly when he did that, something she'd not noticed until now. "Since we are speaking honestly tonight, milady ... I also have a confession to make." He lifted his tankard to his lips and took a deep draft before continuing. "Two days after their escape from Dunan, I caught up with Lady Leanna and Campbell."

Drew inclined her head at this news. "I'd wager that Campbell wasn't happy to see ye."

Broderick's mouth quirked. "Things were tense initially ... but in the end, I let them go."

Drew smiled. "Of course ye did."

His gaze widened. "Ye aren't surprised? I was yer brother's faithful hound after all."

The self-recrimination in his tone was hard to miss, and Drew's smile faded. "So was Campbell, once. But he changed his allegiances." She studied him, her hands now cupped around her tankard. "I'm glad ye told me this, Broderick," she said softly. "I wish I'd confided in ye the way I did in Campbell, but ye are so hard to read I couldn't be sure that ye wouldn't betray me."

His face tightened, a glimmer of the usual severity returning to his features. "I'd never betray ye, Lady Drew," he murmured. "I'd take my own life first."

The words were softly uttered, barely inaudible, and yet they made Drew's breathing hitch. Broderick's loyalty to her was surprising and humbling. She couldn't imagine what she'd done to merit it.

She was just about to say as much when a shadow fell across their booth.

Drew tore her gaze from Broderick, to see that a huge man with close-cropped dark hair and a short beard loomed over her. He'd been one of those playing knucklebones at the nearby table. She'd barely paid him any attention earlier, yet it was impossible to ignore him now when he stood so close.

An odorous wave of stale sweat and rank ale-breath washed over her.

"Lady Drew," the stranger greeted her. His voice, a low growl, made the fine hair on the back of her neck stand up.

Spine stiffening, Drew met his gaze. "Do we know each other?"

"No," he drawled. "Ye don't know me … but I know ye well enough. I used to watch ye riding out on hunts with yer brother, with yer nose stuck in the air like ye were too good for the rest of us."

Cold washed over Drew. The hostility in the man's voice was impossible to miss. The urge to flick a pleading glance in Broderick's direction rose within her, but she forced it down. She wasn't the sort of woman to let a man intimidate her. She'd stood up to Duncan enough times over the years—even knowing he'd strike her for voicing her opinion. She wouldn't let this man cow her.

However, she didn't answer him. She merely held his gaze, waiting for him to back away from the booth.

He didn't.

"The lady is occupied," Broderick spoke up then, his voice cool and dispassionate. "I suggest now that ye have made yer greetings ye leave her to finish her supper in peace."

The stranger ignored the guard, his gaze never straying from Drew.

"Duncan MacKinnon wronged me and my kin," he growled. "He hanged my brother for poaching his deer, and he emptied our stores of grain so that we all nearly starved two winters ago."

Drew swallowed. She was sorry to hear that, yet voicing such sympathies wasn't appropriate here. This man hadn't come for an apology.

"My Da got so thin after the lean winter that he sickened and died," the stranger continued. "With his dying breath, he begged me to make MacKinnon pay for what he did to us."

Drew's breathing slowed, foreboding feathering down her spine. Indeed, this man had good reason to bear a grudge.

The man leaned toward her, his odor almost overpowering. "I always swore I'd have my reckoning upon him," he growled, "but the weasel went and got himself killed before I had the chance."

Drew still didn't say a word. There was nothing she could say that wouldn't make her look insincere. She could feel this man's hostility emanating off him in waves now. Behind him, she saw his friends at the table rise to their feet and move toward him. All eyes in the common room now seemed fixed upon Lady Drew and her guard.

Likewise though, Broderick's six warriors abandoned the remains of their suppers and tankards of ale and stood up.

Even the harpist had stopped playing.

Drew's heart began to thud against her ribs. *Lord, no ... they're going to start a brawl.*

"No fighting in here," the innkeeper called out from across the room. There was a shrill edge to his voice. "Take it outside."

"Nothing to say, eh, Lady Drew?" The stranger's mouth twisted. He ignored the innkeeper, ignored everyone except Drew. The intensity of his stare made a lump form in the pit of her belly. "I thought ye would be feistier ... but ye will react soon enough."

With that, a meaty hand shot out, grabbed her by the upper arm, and hauled her out of the booth. "Duncan MacKinnon is out of my reach now, but ye aren't. Tonight ye shall be my whore ... upstairs with ye!"

6

An Enigma

CHAOS ERUPTED WITHIN *The King's Arms.*

Carr Broderick launched himself from his seat, and his men pounced too. Fists flew and rough shouts boomed up into the rafters. The harpist let out a shriek and cowered against the wall.

"No fighting in here! No fighting!" The innkeeper yelled, his voice barely audible above the din.

A wave of dizziness crashed over Drew, her breathing coming in panicked gulps. Her attacker's grip on her arm was bruising as he towed her across the floor. However, a moment later he released her, for Broderick barreled into him, knocking him back across the nearby table. Knucklebones and tankards of ale scattered, yet Broderick was oblivious.

He went straight for Drew's assailant's throat.

Drew staggered, fear turning her limbs to porridge. She lurched toward the booth, crawling back into it in an effort to get out of the fracas. Her fingers curled around the knife she'd been using to cut up her supper. If that man came at her again, she'd use it on him.

But it appeared that Broderick had the situation under control.

She'd never seen her guard in a real fight before. She had watched him spar with the other warriors in the bailey a few times over the years and knew he was quick on his feet, but his savagery now shocked her.

Despite that the man who'd attacked her was well over six-foot, dwarfing most men in the room, Broderick had him pinned to the table and was slamming his fist repeatedly into his face. Around him, the rest of her escort were grappling with the man's friends.

One of them grabbed a knife and went for a MacKinnon guard with it. However, the warrior—a young guard named Aidan—side-stepped him, grabbed him by the wrist, and hauled him close before head-butting him.

The man went down like a sack of barley, sprawling upon the sawdust.

Moments later it was over.

Breathing hard, Broderick pushed himself up off the table and hauled the now unconscious man with him by the scruff. Meanwhile, the rest of Drew's escort had downed the other trouble-makers.

"Apologies for the brawl," Broderick panted, meeting the innkeeper's eye. The man had gone red in the face and wore a frantic expression. "But as ye saw, we didn't start it." He made for the door, hauling the unconscious man across the sawdust behind him. "Everyone can go back to their ales ... the lads and I will clear this up."

Drew watched him and the rest of her escort gather up the band who'd attacked them before they dragged them outside.

The shocked looks on the faces of the other patrons were almost comical—or they would have been if Drew could see the humorous side of all of this.

She couldn't.

Heart pounding like a battle drum, she relaxed her death-grip on the knife.

She knew that her brother had been hated, but she hadn't realized till this evening just how much ill-will some of the people of this land bore him—and her.

Just another reason why I have to leave Skye, she told herself. *Craeg needs to make a fresh start, one without my presence tainting everything.* As her attacker had so candidly pointed out, most folk associated her with Duncan MacKinnon, and they always would.

Gaze scanning the common room, Drew saw that the innkeeper and a serving lass were righting tables and chairs and scooping up broken tankards.

Drew met the innkeeper's eye. She could tell from his red face and pinched mouth that he was fuming, and likely blamed her for the brawl. "I really am sorry about this," she said, her voice unnaturally loud in the now silent common room. Surveying the curious faces and probing stares, Drew offered them all a weak smile.

"Another round of ale for everyone, please," she said, catching the innkeeper's eye once more as she dug into her purse and held up a silver penny. "And a jug of yer best wine at this table too when ye have a moment."

"This wine's got a kick like a pony," Broderick said, setting his empty goblet down on the table. He then favored Drew with a lopsided smile. "I don't suppose there's any left?"

"I think so." Drew picked up the jug and filled his goblet before topping up her own. "It's bramble ... delicious."

Drew was aware then that she'd almost slurred that last word. The wine—dark and spicy—was indeed strong. Despite that she had a belly full of food, it had made her woozy. Her head spun, and her limbs felt weak and languorous. A warm glow lit her from within.

The evening hadn't started well, admittedly. But now that the trouble-makers had been turfed out, and Broderick had returned to her booth, things had improved.

The common room had emptied as the evening wore on. Two of Broderick's men were playing Ard-ri by the fire, moving carven pieces across a board, while the other guards had retired for the evening. The innkeeper was washing tankards in sudsy water at the far end of the room, and the serving lass was now starting to wipe down tables—a signal that it was getting late.

However, Drew didn't feel like vacating this booth just yet.

She was enjoying sitting in comfort, chatting to Broderick like he was an old friend.

When he'd returned from outdoors, he'd worn a formidable expression—one so severe that she'd thought the worst.

"Did ye kill him?" she asked, dreading the answer.

Broderick had shaken his head. "Why … did ye want me to?"

"No," Drew had replied quickly. "It's just that the look on yer face is murderous."

"I *wanted* to end him," he'd answered, his voice soft yet with an underlying note of steel that had made her suppress a shudder. "If he'd harmed ye, I would have."

The answer had been brutally direct, and for a moment, Drew had fallen silent, not sure how to respond.

Broderick's protectiveness over her made her both feel flustered and flattered. Finally, instead of answering him, she'd gestured to the jug that sat at her right elbow. "Wine?"

Two jugs of wine later, Drew knew she was reaching her limits. If she drank much more, she'd likely sprawl on her face the moment she tried to get up from the booth. Not lady-like at all.

Broderick, however, seemed unaffected. Only the relaxed lines of his face, the slight gleam to his blue-grey eyes, betrayed him.

As the evening wore on, and they chatted amicably about the events of the last few months, Drew found herself observing the man seated across from her.

Broderick wore a cream-colored léine, open at the neck, and Drew's attention kept straying to that opening, where dark gold curls peeked over the top of the garment.

Dreamily, she wondered what the rest of his chest looked like, under the tunic.

Good Lord, ye really have over-indulged on the wine, Drew checked herself. Even so, her gaze still lingered upon him.

"Carr," she said finally, enjoying the sound of his first name on her lips. She usually addressed him by his family name, but this evening the wine had relaxed her formality around him. "All these years ye have served my family ... and I know very little about ye."

He reclined back in his seat, watching her. "What would ye like to know, milady?"

"Yer kin ... where are they?"

His mouth lifted at the corners. "All over Scotland these days ... but my kin hail from Cork, in Éire. I was born there."

"And do yer parents still live? Do ye have any siblings?"

He lifted the goblet to his lips and took a measured sip. "My parents died years ago. I'm the youngest of six sons. My father was once a wealthy man, a land-owner in Cork, but he spent every last bit of silver he possessed on finery, rich food ... and women. He died a pauper."

Drew raised her eyebrows. This tale was getting more interesting by the moment. "So ye set off to seek yer own fortune?"

He nodded, meeting her eye. His expression was veiled. Carr Broderick was definitely a hard man to read.

"No wonder ye and Campbell became friends," she said after a pause. "Ye are both the youngest sons of big families, forced to make yer own way in the world."

Broderick huffed a soft laugh. "We've always had that in common, aye."

Drew took a sip from her goblet, still holding his gaze. It was strange really, but the more she learned about Broderick this evening, the more he fascinated her.

Why haven't we ever spoken like this before?

The answer was simple enough, she supposed. Their positions at Dunan had been vastly different. While they'd lived there, she'd seen him only as one of her brother's warriors.

"Ye are quite an enigma, Carr Broderick," she admitted. "A man who never lets the world see what he's thinking."

He laughed once more, although his gaze turned watchful. "Aye … but there's wisdom in that, Lady Drew."

Her mouth quirked. "But haven't ye ever wanted to take a wife … to have a family? It seems a lonely life ye have chosen."

As soon as the words were out, she wished she could have chased them back into her mouth. Even for her, the question was too bold, too personal.

Broderick leaned back, his fingers sliding up and down the stem of his goblet. Breaking eye contact with him, Drew stared down at his hands. They were big but surprisingly graceful for a man of his broad build.

Blinking hard, Drew forced her gaze back up to his face. The wine was loosening her up far too much.

"Ye are right, milady," he said finally. His tone was measured, neutral, giving no clue as to whether she'd offended him or not. "There have been times when I have questioned the road I've taken … but my life in The Dunan Guard was important to me. Until a few months ago, my loyalty to yer brother was unshakable."

"But ye appear to live like a monk. Why?"

Once again, the words were too bold, and the moment they slid off her tongue, Drew clamped her jaw shut.

That's it, she vowed. *No more wine for me.*

This time, Broderick smiled—and it was a slow, sensual expression that made Drew grow still. "What makes ye think I live like a monk?"

7

Stolen Moments

"WELL, I'VE NEVER seen ye with a woman," Drew replied. She deliberately injected a teasing edge to her voice, even as heat crept up her neck. "I assumed that—"

"I'm discreet," he replied, still smiling.

Drew could see the challenge in his eye now. He was daring her to push on.

"Who then?" she asked casually. She leaned back and took a sip of wine as if his answer mattered not to her.

"Kenzie."

Drew's lips parted in surprise. "The kitchen maid?"

"Aye ... there is none other of that name in the broch."

Kenzie was one of the few kitchen servants who'd remained after the sickness had swept through Dunan. Small, with hair the color of ripe wheat, and warm blue eyes, Drew could see why Broderick might like her.

Even so, Drew favored her guard with an amused smile. "Really?"

He raised an eyebrow. "Ye are surprised?"

"No," Drew scoffed. "It's just that Kenzie appears such a shy lass."

His eyes twinkled. "Not as timid as she appears. A few months ago, she knocked on my bed-chamber door wearing a cloak and nothing under it."

Drew's breathing caught. For the first time during their conversation, he'd succeeded in unsettling her. She couldn't believe that Kenzie, the kitchen lass, had the courage to do something so bold.

For all her flirting, Drew had never acted so recklessly. Something deep inside her chest drew tight as she wished she had. She'd lived such a dull life in many ways.

Drew lifted her goblet and held it up to Broderick in a toast. "Well, here's to a happy union between ye both ... have ye set a wedding date yet?"

Her guard shook his head. He was observing her now with an odd look on his face as if he was trying to gauge her mood. "Kenzie and I aren't together, milady. It was one night ... and stopped there."

Drew inclined her head. "Why is that?"

As she held his gaze, Drew saw a veil fall over Broderick's eyes. "Some encounters are best left to just one occasion," he replied, his tone guarded. "Kenzie and I both decided that it was for the best."

Carr followed Drew up the stairs, his steps heavy.

What had been one of the memorable evenings of his life had ended uncomfortably.

I can't believe I told Lady Drew about Kenzie.

The wine had lowered his guard, loosened his tongue. He was lucky he hadn't said anything else.

Just as well he hadn't told Lady Drew that he loved her.

Carr's lips pressed together into a hard, thin line as he imagined just how humiliating such a confession would have been.

His thoughts returned then to that eve, a few months earlier, when Kenzie had knocked upon his door. She'd stood in the corridor, her blue eyes gleaming, and had parted the cloak to show her nudity underneath. "Just once, Carr," she'd purred. "I know ye and I can never be … but tonight let us forget that."

After they'd coupled, Kenzie had admitted she knew Carr's heart was already spoken for.

"It's Lady Drew, isn't it?" she asked, propping herself up onto one elbow and observing him frankly. "I've seen the way ye gaze upon her."

A chill had crept over Carr's body at her comment. Satan's cods, was he that obvious?

Kenzie had smiled at the panic that had obviously shown upon his face. "Worry not … I doubt anyone else has noticed. Lady Coira perhaps … although Lady Drew herself is oblivious to it."

Those words had stung, yet they were true. Lady Drew didn't see him as a man. To her, he was 'Broderick': the reserved guard who dogged her steps and curtailed her freedom.

They reached the landing at the top of the stairs, and Lady Drew tripped. She would have fallen against the wall if Carr hadn't leaped forward and caught her around the hips, hauling her back against him.

For the briefest of instants, their bodies were pressed flush together. He felt the slender length of her back against his chest, the curve of her buttocks against his groin.

Heat surged through his lower body, and Carr pushed her away from him, panic clamping around his chest.

The last thing he needed was to humiliate himself right now.

However, Lady Drew hadn't noticed. She gave an embarrassed laugh and tottered away from him.

"Apologies, Broderick … I think I may have over imbibed tonight."

Aye, he thought grimly. She had—they both had.

And yet the words that had passed between them, the lingering looks, were an unexpected gift, stolen moments that Carr couldn't bring himself to regret. He'd treasure them till the end of his days.

Lady Drew stumbled along the hallway and reached a door, her fingers curling around the handle.

"Milady." Carr stepped quickly to her side and drew her back. "That isn't yer bed-chamber."

Drew glanced up, turning her face fully to him, her eyes widening. "It isn't?"

For a long moment, their gazes fused. Carr was aware then of just how close they were standing. They were so near that he could see the fine texture of her skin, the darker flecks of slate against the smoke grey in her eyes. She smelt of rosemary and lavender.

Carr could hear the 'thud' of his heart against his ribs. He was acutely aware too of the fact that his fingers now tingled, for he ached to touch her.

He swallowed. This wasn't good—not at all.

The moment lengthened, and Drew's eyes darkened, the pupils growing large, her Cupid's bow lips parting.

The Lord have mercy. He wasn't made out of stone. This woman's nearness was heady; it had far more effect upon him than bramble wine. A dull ache throbbed under his breastbone, the pain reminding him of just how impossible his yearning for this woman was.

Tonight had been both pleasure and pain, yet he had to put an end to things now before he did something he would seriously regret in the morning.

Lady Drew's senses were addled with wine, her defenses lowered. He wouldn't take advantage of her.

"That room is mine, milady," he said softly, taking a deliberate step back and gently pushing her in the right direction. "Sleep well."

Drew stepped into her bed-chamber and pushed the door closed behind her. Leaning her back against it, she took a deep, steadying breath. Around her, the shadowy room had started to spin. She needed to get to her bed before she fell over.

Lord, that wine has addled my brains.

Had she imagined it, outside in the hallway, or had Carr Broderick almost kissed her?

She'd gazed up into his face and seen hunger in his eyes. Standing so close to him had turned her breathless. His closeness, the warmth of his body, and the scent of leather and musky, virile male had overwhelmed her. She'd leaned into him then, wanting him to lower his lips to hers—yet he hadn't.

Drew raised a trembling hand and touched her mouth. She wished he had kissed her.

This trip from Dunan to Inishail hadn't begun as she'd expected. They hadn't even left Skye, and it had already turned into an adventure. A brawl and a revealing conversation that made her see the man who'd been charged with her protection in a completely different light—tonight was memorable, to say the least.

"I'm feeling unwell."

Lady Drew's comment, muttered between clenched teeth, made Carr glance over at her. He perched at the bow of the barge that was taking them across the water to the mainland.

Carr frowned, taking in her pale face and the lines of tension around her mouth. "It's not long now till we dock, milady," he murmured.

"I'm not sure I can wait till then." As if to make her point, Drew clutched at her belly, her pallor increasing.

Kyle of Lochalsh loomed before them, a cluster of stone cottages with thatched roofs rising out of the mist. Around them, the waters of Loch Carron were dark and still this morning. The crossing wasn't rough at all, although Carr knew that wasn't the reason why the lady was unwell.

Last night's excesses were catching up with her.

The rhythmic splash of the oars was the only sound this morning, for the rest of the escort were silent, huddled into their fur cloaks, and bleary-eyed after such an early start. They'd left their horses, including Lady Drew's palfrey, stabled at *The King's Arms*, and would collect them on their way home.

Their first task upon disembarking at Lochalsh would be to find new mounts in order to continue their journey.

Although he was keeping a wary eye on Lady Drew, Carr didn't make any further comment. Nothing he said was going to ease her roiling belly.

However, the moment the barge docked against the rickety wooden pier, Drew scrambled off the boat and fled a few yards up the dock, before falling to her knees and throwing up over the side.

The sight of her retching, huddled form, made concern well up within Carr.

Thanking the ferryman, and handing him a coin for his trouble, Carr disembarked onto the dock and made his way up to Drew.

"Milady," he began hesitantly. "Are ye well?"

"No," she gasped. "Remind me, Broderick, never to touch wine. Ever. Again."

His mouth curved. "Worry not, milady. Where ye are going, ye will be forced to exercise more temperance."

Drew muttered an unladylike curse under her breath and pushed herself to her feet. She then turned to Carr, fixing him in a gimlet stare he knew well; it was one she usually gave him when he thwarted her.

"Ye should have stopped me from drinking so much," she challenged.

He snorted at that. "I'm yer guard, Lady Drew," he said, his mouth twitching from the effort it was taking not to laugh. "Not yer nurse."

Seeing Drew's gaze narrow, he moved past her and motioned to the other men, who had gathered at the end of the dock. They were yawning and stretching and looked as unmotivated as Drew for the day's journey.

"Come on, ye lazy lot," he called out. "Time to go."

8

I Haven't Lived

DREW HADN'T REALIZED that a headache could pulse in time with her heartbeat, in time with each jolting stride her horse took—yet this one did.

She hadn't lied earlier. She never intended to touch wine again.

Unlike her elder brother, she'd been moderate with strong drink her whole life. She didn't like to have her senses impaired in any way, or to lower her guard. When Duncan was alive, it would have been dangerous to do so—for she always needed to be wary of him.

But last night she'd felt a bit wild. She'd been away from Dunan for the first time in years, and although she'd been scared when that brute had grabbed her, the brawl that had followed had been oddly exciting.

However, in the cold light of a grey winter's morning, with her mouth sour, her belly churning, and her temples pounding, the novelty had faded.

She was back in control, and reality had returned to her world.

She was a widow well past her prime, journeying to a new life as a nun. She shouldn't be downing jugs of wine with her guards.

The company rode east now, following the northern edge of the loch.

Slowly, as the morning drew out, the nausea that bit at the back of Drew's throat and the pain in her head eased. Thirsty, she drained the contents of her water bladder, which the innkeeper had graciously filled with cooled boiled water for her that morning.

She'd been unable to face her bannocks—just the sight and smell of them had nearly made her heave—but as the pale winter sun broke through the heavy canopy of cloud overhead and warmed her face, she felt the stirring of hunger in her belly.

At noon they stopped off upon the shores of the loch at the village of Dornie, where Carr bought bread, cheese, and dried blood sausage. It was market day in Dornie, and the large cobbled square in the heart of the village bustled with life. The bleating, honking, and clucking of livestock rose high into the damp air, vying with the call of vendors.

Seated upon a crate on the edge of the square, Drew took in the busy crowd. Women, with baskets under their arms and plaid cloaks about their shoulders, chatted together as they shopped.

A hollow feeling lodged itself under Drew's ribs as she watched them. She suddenly wished she was one of those women, buying a mutton pie, cheese, and eggs to bring home for her family. The ritual that these farmers' wives took for granted was something Drew longed to experience. A lady didn't take a basket to market—she had servants to do such things for her.

I won't be attending any markets at Inishail either. Coira had told her that abbeys and priories tended to be largely self-sufficient. Even if there was a village nearby, the nuns would likely have little to do with it.

This would possibly be the last market she'd attend.

Brushing crumbs off her skirts, Drew glanced up and caught her guard's eye. "I'd like to take a turn around the square, Broderick."

His mouth compressed. "We should really be on our way, milady."

"I'm sure we have time for this," she replied airily. Rising to her feet, she adjusted her fur mantle about her shoulders. "Stay here, if ye wish. I won't be long."

Of course he didn't stay with the others. Broderick never let her out of his sight back in Dunan, and he certainly wouldn't now that they were traveling together.

Usually, his presence irritated her. But today, now that she was feeling herself again, she found she didn't mind the fact that he walked two steps behind her as she wove her way through the jostling crowd.

Drew stopped before a stall selling cakes and pies. The aroma of the baking made her mouth water, especially when her gaze alighted on a tray of honey cakes. "How many days' journey is it to Inishail?" she asked Broderick, casting a glance over her shoulder.

"Another three at most," he replied, his expression as unreadable as ever. "Once we reach the eastern edge of this loch, we shall head directly south into more mountainous lands."

Three more days.

Drew turned from him, her attention returning to the honey cakes. Suddenly, Inishail loomed on the horizon, more of a dungeon than a sanctuary. Back in Dunan, her destination had seemed far off. "I wish it were farther," she murmured.

"Milady?" Broderick stepped up to her shoulder.

"I've seen so little of the world," she said softly, meeting his eye once more. "Three days isn't long enough. Three weeks would be better."

Breaking eye contact with her guard, she motioned to the woman at the stall that she'd like some cakes.

"How many, *milady*?" the woman asked, a smile stretching her face. Of course, dressed in her fine furs, rings sparkling upon her fingers, Drew stood out in this crowd.

"Eight please," Drew replied.

"Eight?" Broderick rumbled. "Ye have quite an appetite today, Lady Drew."

Drew gave an unladylike snort. "Clod-head, these aren't all for me. I take it ye and the others like honey-cakes?"

"I can't speak for the others, but I'm very partial to them," Broderick replied. His grey-blue eyes crinkling at the corners as his mouth curved.

The expression made Drew's gaze linger upon his face. Carr Broderick was actually quite handsome when he smiled.

Thunder rumbled overhead. The first droplets of rain pattered onto the ground as the company clattered into the tiny white-washed hamlet of Invershiel at dusk. The village sat on the farthest edge of the loch.

Finding lodgings at the only establishment, *The Shiel Inn*, the travelers saw to their horses before going directly to their rooms. After the excitement of the night before, Broderick had insisted they all get an early night.

Drew noted that none of his men objected. They were all as weary as she was.

Seated at a small table in her bed-chamber, listening to the rain drumming against the shutters, Drew ate her supper of venison stew and oaten dumplings alone.

A hollow sensation settled within her as she ate, despite her rapidly filling belly.

She knew that the night before couldn't be repeated; she and Broderick had been far too frank with each other. But, all the same, she missed his company.

Goose, she chided herself, putting down her spoon and pushing away the remains of her supper. *Ye and Broderick will soon part ways ... ye need to get used to not having him nearby.*

Her breathing slowed as she dwelled on that thought. For months now, she'd been irritated by his constant presence. But now the thought of saying goodbye to Broderick saddened her.

She wanted to travel with him for a while, chat with him long into the night at smoky inns, tease him until he smiled, and look on while he and his men dealt with troublemakers again.

All of a sudden, she wanted a little unpredictability, a little danger, in her life. Soon she'd be in a place where every moment of her day would adhere to a strict routine. But she wasn't there yet. There was still time for some excitement.

Drew rose from the stool and started to pace the scrubbed wooden floor of her bed-chamber. However, the act soon made her dizzy, for the room was tiny. There was nowhere to go.

I haven't lived.

Until now, she'd lived a restricted life. But out here on the road, she'd tasted what freedom might feel like. The last two days had awakened something in her, a longing that refused to be quietened. She was like a bird loosed from its cage—she wanted some adventure before she entered a new prison.

A heaviness settled within Drew then. She sank down upon the bed and listened to the howling wind and rain outdoors. Inishail inched ever closer. It was too late now to wish for excitement.

Drew was unusually silent when they set off the next morning. She noted that Broderick, and one or two of the other men, kept glancing her way while they saddled their horses. Although not a woman given to prattle, Lady Drew usually embraced the morning.

She liked to greet her escort and comment on what the weather might hold for the day's journey.

Yet this morning, she kept her own counsel.

"Are ye well, milady?" Aidan asked. "Ye are very pale this morning."

Drew pursed her lips and allowed the young warrior to help her up onto her mount, a leggy courser they'd hired at Lochalsh. The beast was spirited and a far less comfortable ride than the sweet-tempered palfrey she'd left behind at Kyleakin.

"I'm well, thank ye."

It was a lie. She felt tense and tired. She'd barely slept overnight. Instead, she'd lain for hours, staring up at the darkness, wondering at how she'd managed to reach thirty-six winters without truly living.

Long, hard years stretched before her, and yet she had few memories to sustain her.

Adjusting her skirts, Drew glanced up to find Broderick watching her. He'd mounted his horse and waited in the center of the dirt yard behind the inn. "If ye wish, we can take more rests today, milady," he said after a pause. "I don't want to deliver ye to Inishail Priory unwell."

Drew cast him an imperious look, her spine stiffening as she squared her shoulders. "I'm not made of silk," she reminded him. "I don't need to take more rests."

Broderick raised a dark-blond eyebrow. "Ready to ride out then, milady?"

Drew nodded. Despite that she was already weary, she welcomed being out in the fresh air and on the road. There was a restlessness within her this morning that made her want to give her horse its head. She wanted to gallop into the wilds and never return.

Urging the courser forward, she rode past Broderick and out into Invershiel's only street: an unpaved way with deep ruts. It was a blustery winter's morning, with a wind howling in from the north. The village folk she passed had red cheeks from the wind's stinging chill, but the rainclouds of the day before had cleared. This morning, white clouds chased each other across a pale blue sky.

Not bothering to glance behind her to see if her escort was following, Drew nudged the courser into a brisk trot.

Then, turning onto the highway, she urged her spirited mount forward. The courser kicked up its heels and sprang forward into a fast canter.

Moments later another horse pulled up alongside.

Drew glanced over to see that Broderick now rode shoulder-to-shoulder with her. "In a hurry this morning?" he asked, raising his voice to be heard over the thunder of their horses' hooves.

Drew grinned at him. Just this brief spurt of speed had lightened her mood. "Aye ... this gelding chafed at the bit yesterday, so I thought I'd let him stretch his legs."

To her surprise, Broderick grinned back, a gleam in his eye. "And there was me thinking ye were trying to outrun us all."

Their gazes held for an instant, and then Drew swung her attention back to the open road before them.

An idea rose within her then—a thought so outrageous that her breathing stalled, her fingers clenching around the reins. Her already racing heart started to pound in her ears.

Heat flooded through her lower belly as the idea grew, taking shape fully in her mind.

No, she couldn't be so bold. She was about to enter a priory; she shouldn't even be entertaining such thoughts. She'd never behaved recklessly with men. Now certainly wasn't the time to begin.

And yet now that the idea had seeded in her mind, it would not die.

She remembered then the desire she'd seen darken Carr Broderick's gaze as he'd stood with her outside his room in *The King's Arms*. If she bade him, would he kiss her?

If I asked him, would he lie with me?

9

Tonight

WHEN THEY STOPPED at noon, Drew felt sick with nerves and excitement.

After the initial burst of speed, both she and Broderick had slowed their mounts, pacing themselves for the long day's journey. The highway had taken them south. They traveled across wild moor for a spell before entering a highland region. Bulky pine-clad mountains rose above them, etched against a windswept sky. These peaks were different to those of Skye, Drew reflected. The mountains of her home isle were craggier, almost brutal in appearance. The landscape upon the mainland had a softer edge to it.

Loosening her horse's girth, and letting it take a brief drink from a highland burn, Drew leaned against the courser's sweaty neck and attempted to draw strength from the beast.

It has to be now, she told herself, gathering her courage as anticipation churned in her belly. *Ye have to ask him.*

Drawing in a deep breath, she turned, her gaze going to where Broderick was handing out bread and cheese to his men. He then approached her.

"It's simple fare again, I'm afraid," he said, "although two of the men will ride ahead and see if they can hunt some game for tonight's meal."

Drew's gaze widened. "We'll be sleeping outdoors?"

"Aye ... there aren't any inns until our destination, so for the next two nights we'll be pitching tents."

Drew frowned. That complicated her plans a little, and for a moment, her resolve faltered. Her courage balanced upon a knife-edge.

"Carr," she said softly, taking the bread and cheese he offered. Her fingers deliberately brushed against his as she did so, and she heard his breathing catch. No, she hadn't imagined it. It was desire she'd seen in his eyes that night. She would press on. "Can I speak to ye alone for a moment?"

He frowned at the question. The others were standing a few feet behind them. The men weren't paying them much attention, for they'd already begun to eat and were bickering gently about what game would be the best to hunt for later in the day.

"This won't take long," Drew continued, moving back from him. She needed to make sure they were safely out of earshot of the others before she said anything.

Wordlessly, Broderick followed her, although his brow was furrowed now. He could sense her tension, and it concerned him.

Leading him over to where a single spruce rose high above them, its blue-green needles bathed in wintry sunlight, Drew turned to Broderick and took in another steadying breath.

God's bones, this was harder than she'd expected. Where was her usual brazen self-confidence?

She'd spent most of the morning going over and over in her head what she'd say to him, how she'd phrase things, and all the ways he could possibly respond. Only, now that Carr Broderick stood before her, and the heady scent of pine enveloped them, she felt flustered and tongue-tied.

"Is something amiss, milady?" he asked, his gaze searching her face.

"No ... aye ... well, not really," she replied, stumbling over her answer. Heat crept into her cheeks. She wasn't doing a good job of this. "The thing is ... this journey has made me reflect on things ... reflect on my life thus far. Quite frankly, it's been dull. I will go to Inishail and follow my mother's example ... but before I do ... I ..." she halted there, struggling to get the words out in a coherent fashion. "Before I do that, I want to live. I wish to enjoy carnal pleasure and ... well ... will ye lie with me?"

Broderick went still at that, his face freezing. An awkward silence stretched out between them, and when he eventually spoke, his voice sounded strangled. "Lady Drew ... I don't think—"

"I've thought this through," she cut him off. He was going to refuse her, and she couldn't let him. "It would only be once ... tonight ... and then we could just pretend it never happened. When we reach Inishail, ye and I will go our separate ways."

"This is folly, milady," he replied, his voice roughening now. "A woman's womb can quicken with a bairn after just one coupling. How would ye explain that to the nuns ... to yer mother?"

A laugh rose within Drew, yet she choked it back. "There's no need to worry about that," she replied with a shake of her head. "Ye forget that I was wed for years and Egan never managed to get me with bairn. I'm barren."

It was an ugly word, one that made Drew's throat close up. How often had Duncan mocked her over her failure to produce children; he'd angered Egan over it too when he'd brought up the subject at mealtimes in the Great Hall.

Silence settled between them once more. The shock on Broderick's face would have made her smile in other circumstances, but not now. She felt as if she'd just handed him a weapon he could so easily wield against her.

"I'm yer guard, Lady Drew," Broderick said finally. There was a pleading note in his voice now, blending with its usual gruffness. "Ye shouldn't be asking this of me."

"Why not?" Heat kindled in Drew's belly as her anger rose. In her head, this conversation had gone quite differently. She'd imagined his initial surprise and then ready agreement. He was staring at her as if she'd just sprouted devil's horns. "Am I distasteful to ye, Carr?"

Carr stared at Lady Drew and resisted the urge to take a step back from her—anything to ease the tension of this moment. He felt light-headed, his chest so tight that it hurt to breathe.

"Don't ask me that, milady," he rasped. "Ye shouldn't—"

"Is that it?" she countered, high spots of color appearing upon her pale cheeks. "Ye can bed a kitchen wench, but the thought of touching me turns yer stomach?"

"Stop it, Drew." He forced the words out. He had to prevent this exchange from escalating. She'd already gone too far. "Ye are wrong ... it's not that I don't desire ye ... it's that I'm yer guard. Craeg charged me with yer protection."

"And Craeg will never know," she replied. Drew's heart-shaped face had gone taut with determination. She wasn't a woman used to being thwarted. "This is between ye and me ... no one else."

Satan strike me down, why is she asking this of me?

Carr felt as if he were hanging off the edge of a cliff, clinging to a rope that was slowly fraying. In just a few moments, he'd be plummeting to the rocks below, and there was nothing he could do about it.

For years he'd dreamed of Lady Drew wanting him. How many times had he taken himself in hand in the quiet of his cramped bed-chamber, alone in the darkness, and brought himself to climax while thinking about her?

But those fantasies had been safe, private.

The things that Lady Drew was saying to him now were dangerous for them both—even more so for him, for this woman had his heart.

And she had no idea.

Lady Drew was asking him to service her like he was a prize stallion she'd chosen to put over her best mare. To her, it was nothing more than an exchange, yet to him, it would be everything.

Did she think he could just plow her and forget?

Drew stepped toward him, closing the gap he'd deliberately created. "I know that I am asking ye to break vows ye take very seriously," she said, her voice soft now, her gaze imploring. "But I will ask no more of ye than this. Lie with me just once, Carr ... please."

Carr swallowed, hard. He hated that she was on the verge of begging him. This wasn't how he wanted to remember Lady Drew. And yet, her nearness was intoxicating. The utter lack of guile upon her face, the way her lips parted, transfixed him. Her breast rose and fell sharply, and she clutched the bread and cheese he'd given her as if her life depended on it.

It was taking everything she had to ask this of him.

Yet she didn't realize what it would cost Carr. That wasn't her fault though—he'd been careful to keep his feelings hidden from her.

Letting out a slow exhale, Carr resisted the urge to reach out, to trace the determined line of her jaw with his fingertips. His gut twisted then. It would already be hard enough to leave her at Inishail and ride away, knowing their paths would never cross again.

After this, he'd be broken—inside where no one would see. But, he'd have one memory to treasure, to hold close as the years passed.

"Very well," he murmured, his voice barely audible over the roar of the wind through the overhanging spruce. "Tonight?"

Drew's eyes darkened, her pupils dilating so wide that her irises turned completely black. She then bit her plump lower lip.

Lust jolted through Carr's groin, a sensation so sharp that his breath caught. Heat spread through his limbs, making him feel feverish. God, how he wanted to take hold of her, then and there, pull her behind this spruce, lay her down upon the mossy ground, and give her the servicing she so desperately wanted.

Instead, he clenched his jaw, suffering the ache in his groin, and watched as she nodded and took an unsteady step back from him. "Tonight," Drew agreed softly, before she turned and walked back to the horses.

10

The Waiting

DREW HAD NEVER known a day to pass so slowly.

She'd barely been able to eat her bread and cheese. Her belly had closed in excitement—and as the sun traveled across the sky, that anticipation grew.

She'd done it. She asked him, and now Carr Broderick would lie with her. She was relieved he'd agreed. There had been a point in their conversation when she'd been sure he'd refuse her.

But now that he hadn't, she felt as giddy as a lass at her first dance.

It was silly really, yet she liked the recklessness that had caught fire in her veins since leaving Skye. If she was going to become a nun, she might as well know what she was giving up.

All her life she'd flirted with men, danced around them like a colorful butterfly, enjoying the game. She'd lived as if she had a hundred years to waste. But time was running out now, and she'd not let this opportunity slip through her fingers.

She and Carr barely spoke for the whole afternoon. She let him and Aidan ride ahead, and kept her own counsel. However, she was now acutely aware of him, and her gaze kept returning to his broad shoulders.

It would happen tonight. Her belly flip-flopped at the thought. When and where, she didn't know—but he'd agreed, and that was all that mattered.

Finally, the gloaming arrived. Two of the men who'd ridden ahead to hunt returned with a brace of grouse, which they plucked and roasted over hot coals while the others made camp for the night.

They set up their tents upon a hillside, next to a stand of old oaks. A creek bubbled its way over mossy stones at the bottom of the hill, and Drew collected a pot of water to boil over the fire. They'd need to refill their water bladders at some point.

The semi-circle of tents sat above the fire pit, with Drew's tent—the biggest of the group—sitting at the back.

While the grouse were cooking, Drew found herself growing agitated. Nerves danced in her belly like a party of over-excited brownies. She needed to keep busy, needed to keep her mind focused on other matters. Deciding she would sort through her belongings, she carried her saddlebags into the tent.

Carr was there already, rolling out a fur onto the ground. He glanced up when she entered, and their gazes fused for an instant.

"Will ye come to me here later?" she asked, favoring him with a coy smile.

Carr shook his head, a muscle flexing in his jaw. "It's too near the others ... they might hear something." He paused then, his throat bobbing. "I'll be taking the first watch after supper. When I finish it, I will fetch ye, and we will go to the oak wood together."

Drew's breathing quickened. "But ... how will we—"

"I've removed the pegs behind me." He motioned to the far edge of the tent, the side nearest the woods. "I'll lift the hide ... there will be enough space for ye to squeeze through."

Drew nodded, her heart galloping now. This calm explanation of how they would get time alone together was causing her already churning belly to somersault.

They were whispering together like conspirators; the excitement of it was dizzying.

Carr moved toward the exit behind Drew but stopped when he was level with her. He'd stooped, to avoid hitting his head on the roof of the tent, and as such their faces were much closer than they'd have been usually.

Drew's breath hitched in her chest when she saw the gleam in his eyes, the look of rapt attention as he gazed upon her face. She'd never had a man look upon her so intently; it made her feel dizzy.

Heart pounding, she swallowed. "I shall see ye later then?"

"Aye," he murmured. "Are ye sure about this, Lady Drew?"

She nodded, smiling once more. "Please dispense with formalities, Carr," she whispered back. "This eve, just call me 'Drew'."

His eyes hooded, and Drew realized that, like her, he was breathing faster than normal. Like her, he could feel the charge between them. It was like the air was heavy with the promise of rain, and at any moment a storm would explode.

Warmth spread through Drew's belly, and the sensitive skin between her thighs began to ache.

The waiting was going to kill her.

Carr ate his supper without tasting a morsel. Under normal circumstances, he quite liked grouse, enjoyed the gamey flavor and the char of the meat cooked over hot coals. But this evening, his hunger had waned.

A cold, windy dusk settled over the hillside, making the flames in the small fire pit flare and gutter. The party huddled around it, picking flesh off the grouses they'd cooked.

Wiping the grease off his fingers, Carr glanced across the fire pit at where Lady Drew—Drew—sat. He couldn't get used to even thinking of her by her first name only, let alone hailing her by it.

But since they were about to get as intimate as it was possible for a man and woman, he needed to practice.

Drew looked lovely tonight, bonnier than he'd ever seen her.

Perhaps it was excitement, anticipation of the night ahead, but there was a healthy rouge to her cheeks and her grey eyes were bright and alive as she licked her fingers clean.

Carr swallowed at the sight. She had no idea how sensual that gesture was, especially after the conversations they'd had today.

Shrouded in a fur mantle, Drew perched upon a log and shared a funny story with the two men seated to her right. Her finely boned, yet expressive, hands danced while she told the tale, which had both warriors guffawing loudly at the end of it.

Grinning, Drew sat back, and then, as if feeling his gaze upon her, she looked across the fire at Carr. Her smile faded, although her eyes still danced.

Their gazes locked, and an ache rose under Carr's breastbone.

The Lord strike him down, how was he supposed to resist her when she looked at him like that; those grey eyes promised him the world. This woman would be his ruin.

Alone in her tent, Drew felt the urge to pace—but the tent wasn't large enough to allow it. The restlessness inside her was almost unbearable now.

Instead, she sat upon the furs, listening to the whine of the wind and the rumble of men's voices that punctured the night.

They should be all going to bed soon.

She certainly hoped so, for impatience thrummed through her.

Although the wind was up, the night was mild for this time of year. As such, the warriors who'd accompanied

Carr were, unfortunately, in no hurry to retreat from the fireside.

Drew clenched her jaw and forced herself to breathe. *Patience ... the time will come soon enough.*

Glancing down, she took in the clothing she'd chosen for this occasion. She'd removed her heavy fur mantle, as it would only hinder her when she slipped out of the tent later. Instead, she wore a cream-colored léine with a pine-green kirtle atop it.

Drew's mouth curved into a half-smile as she reached out and traced her fingers over the soft fabric.

Foolish vanity ... he won't even notice what ye are wearing in the dark. Even more foolish too, for soon these fine clothes would be nothing but a memory.

Life at Inishail would strip all her finery from her. At the priory, she'd be the same as everyone else. However, it was something she actually welcomed.

She knew that many of the poor who lived upon MacKinnon lands had viewed her with resentment and jealousy, yet a life of privilege hadn't brought her any more happiness.

She'd never felt as alive as she did in this very moment. Maybe it was because she knew everything was going to change for her soon. The realization had slowed time down, had made her take notice of things she'd only ever taken for granted—like the softness of the finely made léine against her sensitive skin and the luxuriousness of the fur she sat upon.

Swallowing, Drew reached up and unpinned her hair. It tumbled down over her shoulders in soft waves. She usually wore it up, tightly coiled upon the crown of her head. But tonight such a style was too prim, too controlled.

Tonight she was a different woman.

11

In the Moonlight

IT WAS LATE when Carr finally fetched her. So late that Drew had actually lain down upon the furs and fallen into a light doze.

At the sound of someone whispering her name, she sat up, blinking.

The tiny fire pit in the center of the tent had burned down to glowing coals, yet she could just make out Carr's face as he lifted up the edge of the weather-stained hide.

Heart pounding, Drew moved.

Wordlessly, she went to him, took the hand he offered, and squeezed under.

As she rose to her feet, Drew felt nervousness flutter up under her ribcage. This was finally happening; it almost seemed surreal.

Outdoors, the wind buffeted against her, and she glanced up at the sky. There was a full moon tonight. It appeared as the racing clouds parted, allowing hoary light to filter over the world below.

Shifting her attention back to Carr, she saw that the moonlight now kissed the strong lines of his face. However, his eyes were cast into shadow.

He squeezed her hand then and turned, leading her into the oak wood. His hand was warm and strong in hers.

Drew didn't dare glance back at their camp. She knew one of the men would be still awake, keeping watch by the fire. But if they were quiet, he'd never know that they'd crept away.

Moonlight now frosted the trees. Carr didn't speak as he led her deep into the woods, and when they were at least five furlongs distant from the camp, he halted.

Drew's heart was now beating so hard that she could feel it pulsing in her ears. Earlier she'd been all aflutter with excitement. But now she felt sick with nerves. In her head, this encounter had been much less *real*. But now that she and Carr were finally alone together—now that he stared down at her with hunger etched across his features—she suddenly felt out of her depth.

And when Carr dipped his head to kiss her, she took a step back.

"What is it?" he murmured, the rough edge of need in his voice turning her knees weak.

Drew stared at him, her body going taut as a bowstring. Aye, she was in deep water here and floundering badly.

She wasn't sure she could bear it.

And so she turned from him, bracing her hands against the trunk of the massive oak that now towered above them. Moonlight shone down through its supplicating branches, making Drew's fingers, splayed across the rough bark, look so pale they appeared ethereal.

"Take me, Carr," she gasped. "Like this."

Carr didn't know how to react.

For a few moments, he merely stood there, staring at the back of Drew's head. He could hear the soft pant of her breathing and the rasp of his own.

His ribs tightened, his belly clenching in disappointment.

Was this what she wanted ... to be taken like a whore? Drew deserved better than that. He ached to kiss her, longed to trace her lips with the tip of his tongue, to taste the sweetness of her hot mouth—but she was denying him that.

He wouldn't force the issue though, for he could feel her nervousness. It rippled off her body in waves, and that surprised him.

Stepping close to her, he let the length of his body press flush against hers. The soft, plaint feel of her made his breathing catch. He couldn't believe that after all these years, he was allowed to touch her.

He reached up then, his fingers delving into her hair. He loved seeing it like this, loose and wild. Tangling his fingers through it, he leaned forward, inhaling its scent. Then, he lifted her hair up, his lips tracing the long line of her neck.

Drew gasped.

Carr stifled a groan; her reaction set his blood aflame.

His lips left a trail, up her neck, to where his tongue traced the shell of her ear.

Drew moaned, arching back against him. He felt the quiver in her body as his hands closed over her slender shoulders, pulling her hard against him.

He might not be able to kiss her mouth, but he'd not make this coupling cold and passionless. He'd show her how her body could sing.

Nestling his erection into the cleft of her buttocks, he slid his hands down from her shoulders to her breasts, cupping them.

The layers of material between them frustrated Carr. He wouldn't be able to have Drew completely naked, yet he needed to get closer to her. His fingers went to the bodice of her kirtle, to the laces there. He loosened them, and the front of the garment sagged open. Underneath, only a léine separated her breasts from him.

Once again, he cupped the soft mounds, grinding himself against her as he did so.

Drew pushed back against him, her breathing coming in short, desperate pants.

Carr brushed his thumbs over the hard buds of her nipples, his breathing hitching when she gave a soft mewing cry. Carr adored that sound. They were far from the camp now; she could make a little noise.

"Carr," she groaned his name in a plea. "Please ... I need ye."

Stifling a groan of his own, Carr continued to stroke her nipples with the pad of his thumbs. He then gently tweaked them, his shaft aching as she arched back against him, her supple body shuddering.

He then slid his hands down the length of her torso, over her belly to her hips, where he grabbed handfuls of her skirts and pulled them up. Nudging her legs apart with a knee, he slid his fingers between her thighs.

He then groaned.

She was so wet, so ready for him.

Slowly, he stroked her there, his heart thundering in his ears when she started to gasp and rotate her hips against his groin.

He couldn't stand it. He'd planned to take this slow, to pleasure her for a while yet before he took her, but the fire in his blood was raging out of control now.

All he could think about was being inside her.

With his free hand, he reached down and unlaced his braies, releasing his engorged shaft. And then, he stepped back from her, raising her skirts high so that they bunched around her waist.

The twin globes of her buttocks gleamed in the moonlight, and he stroked them, marveling at the smoothness of her skin.

It was as if his lustiest dreams had suddenly come to life. Drew was heart-stoppingly sensual. She was panting loudly now, pushing her exposed rear toward him.

A low growl rose in Carr's throat. How did she expect him to go slowly when she did that?

Taking hold of her hips, he raised her up, placing the tip of his shaft at her core's entrance—and then he entered her in one slow, deep movement.

Drew's hoarse cry echoed through the trees.

They shouldn't really make too much noise, for, despite their distance from camp, sounds carried in the night, but Carr was past caring at this point.

She was so hot, so tight, he almost lost control, then and there.

Drew bucked against him, yet he gripped her hips tightly, holding her still as he withdrew almost completely and then plunged into her once more.

He took her like that—in long, hard thrusts—while she writhed and shuddered. Her heat contracted around him, and he felt a rush of wetness as his shaft stroked deep within her.

"Carr," she gasped, when he thrust deep once more, her voice raw, beseeching. "It's too much ... please stop!"

12

Not Enough

TO DREW'S SURPRISE, he halted.

She'd thought him too far gone to listen to her, thought that he'd just continue to plow her until he found his own release—but Carr had heard Drew's plea, and he stilled, still buried deep inside her.

Suddenly, the only noise in the oak wood, besides the whistling of the wind and the creak of branches, was their rough breathing.

An ache rose in Drew's breast then, as disappointment filtered through her. It had been too intense; she'd been on the brink of losing control. But now that he'd stilled, she wanted him to ignore her—to plow her until she fainted.

He didn't say a word, slowly withdrawing from her.

Drew's throat thickened at the feeling of loss. How she loved having him inside her. When he'd first entered her, his size had been a shock. Her husband had never stretched her like that, had never turned her loins molten.

Drew closed her eyes, tears stinging her eyelids.

Goose, she chided herself. *Yer one chance to let go and ye have ruined it.*

Yet, Carr didn't release her and step away, as she'd expected. Instead, he gently turned her around to face him.

Moments slid by, and then he took hold of her chin and lifted it so that their gazes met. Drew's breathing caught; the fierce look of tenderness and desire that played across his shadowed features was almost too much to bear.

"Do ye trust me, Drew?" he asked, his voice husky now.

"Aye," she whispered.

"Tell me what ye want, and I'll do as ye wish."

Drew swallowed, her heart galloping as the pad of his thumb softly traced her lower lip. He was giving her the chance to end this if that was what she truly wanted. He was letting her choose.

"Carr," she breathed his name, reaching up and tracing his jaw with a trembling hand. For one night she needed to be wild and reckless—to let go. "Claim me," she whispered.

Carr's breathing caught, and for an instant, he went still. And then he moved.

He gathered her up and took two steps forward, bringing her hard up against the oak trunk. He then kneed her trembling thighs apart and drove into her.

And this time, as he did so, his mouth claimed hers.

He kissed her wildly; his lips and tongue ravaging, demanding.

Drew didn't think, didn't analyze. Instead, she responded with a hunger equal to his. Somehow facing him, kissing him, made her fear ebb. She felt reassured. Reaching up, she wound her arms around his neck, pulling him closer still, the aching tips of her breasts rubbing against the leather of his vest.

He took Drew slowly, purposefully, grinding his hips against hers in a sensual dance that had her clinging to him.

Trembling like a leaf in the wind, Drew held on. She'd thought the last position had been wonderful, but this one was even better. The intimacy of it made her ache for him unbearable. He filled her. The taste and smell of him overwhelmed her senses.

The sensual slide of Carr's tongue against hers as he thrust into her was too much, and Drew spun out of control. She clutched at him and cried out against his mouth, yet this time he didn't stop. This time he plowed her hard until his body shuddered and arched against Drew, his mouth bruising hers.

Drew clung to him in the aftermath, gasping while the pleasure ebbed and a melting sensation suffused her body. She'd never felt so relaxed, so at peace in the moment. Nestling her face into his neck, she breathed in his warm, musky male scent. She placed a hand upon Carr's chest then, her fingers spreading out over his racing heart.

Awe swept over her, the sensation so powerful that tears pricked her eyelids and a lump rose in her throat. He was still buried inside her, and she never wanted him to leave.

"That was wonderful," she whispered, tracing feather-light kisses over the hollow of his throat. "Can we do it again?"

Laughter rumbled through Carr's chest, and she felt his grip around her tighten. "Aye," he rasped. "Just give me a few moments."

Stretching languorously, Drew opened her eyes before rolling over onto her back. The first glimmers of dawn peeked through the smoke hole in the roof above her.

A dull ache pulsed between her thighs, yet her body had never felt so good. A smile spread across her face. She now understood why Coira gazed at Craeg with that secret, soft look—why she blushed when he lowered his mouth to her ear and whispered to her.

Until last night she'd always believed coupling to be an uncomfortable, animalistic urge. She'd never known that it could strip away the rest of the world, make all her worries and cares meaningless.

For a short time, she and Carr had been the only two people alive. And she'd wanted him like she needed air.

Drew's eyes flickered open, and she pushed herself up. The murmur of men's voices warned her that she couldn't lie here any longer. Carr and his warriors were packing up, and shortly they would continue on their journey south.

Inishail Priory was only two days' ride away.

The veil of contentment that had shrouded Drew for hours fell away, and her smile faded.

That was it. Carr has given ye a memory to treasure, but it ends here.

A heaviness settled over her then, as the full force of the realization hit her. She was greedy for more of him. She wanted to have days and days alone with Carr Broderick. She wanted to undress that strong body, to explore his skin with her lips, tongue, and fingertips.

Last night wasn't enough.

Drew's mouth compressed then.

It will have to be.

Getting to her feet, she grabbed the edge of the fur and started rolling it up. Sometimes she tired of herself— of her selfish will that railed against the confines of the life she'd been given. She had to quash it.

Last night had been a gift. However, Carr wasn't hers and soon they'd part ways forever. She needed to remember that.

Fool.

Carr swallowed a mouthful of twice-baked oatcake and glared at the smoking remains of last night's fire.

He should have known this would happen; it would have been obvious to anyone else. He was already sick with love for Drew MacKinnon, and last night had turned that sickness into a raging fever that now consumed him.

Being inside her, touching her, kissing her—it had unleashed a part of him that could no longer be caged.

I can't let her take the veil.

Yet Lady Drew didn't belong to him. He'd agreed to last night, knowing that it wouldn't be repeated. But having a taste of the woman he loved, the woman who dominated his every waking thought, had broken through his usual self-control and reserve.

He couldn't bear it.

A flash of movement to his left caught Carr's eye. Glancing up, he watched Drew emerge from her tent, and try as he might to prevent his physical reaction, his breathing caught.

Unlike the night before, her peat-brown hair was now braided and coiled tightly upon her crown. However, the style exposed her swanlike neck—a neck that he'd kissed and tasted.

Carr's pulse quickened, and he tore his gaze away, looking down at the half-eaten oatcake.

Suddenly, he had no appetite for it.

"Lady Drew." He tossed away the oatcake and rose to his feet as she neared the smoldering fire pit. Around them, the other men were taking down the tents. He should be helping, but this morning, all he could do was stare at this woman like a lackwit. "Can I speak to ye for a moment ... alone?"

His jaw clenched when he finished speaking, for his question reminded him of the one she'd asked him the day before at noon.

How much had changed since then.

Drew halted, her grey eyes widening as their gazes fused. She stared at him, her lovely face tensing. Then, warily, she nodded.

He led her over to where the horses waited, tied to trees on the edge of the oak wood. Even being near this place, the secret spot where he'd taken Drew up against a tree, made Carr's pulse accelerate.

Not thinking, not allowing himself to dwell on what he was about to do—lest his courage fail him—Carr turned to Drew.

She stopped, around three feet away from him. Close enough that he could have reached for her if he'd wanted, could have hauled her into his arms and kissed her for all the world to see.

The need to do so was a dull ache in his chest.

"Drew," he whispered.

Her eyes widened. "Isn't it Lady Drew now, Broderick?" she asked, favoring him with a smile. However, the expression was wobbly, forced. He could see by the sharp rise and fall of her breast that she was as affected by his nearness as he was by hers.

"I don't want it to be," he murmured. He was aware of the desperate rasp in his voice, yet he couldn't stop it. He couldn't hold back how he felt anymore. He'd ached to tell her the night before, but instead, he'd led Drew back to her tent, kissed her in the darkness, and then let her return to her bed.

He was running out of chances. Inishail Priory loomed before them, a specter on the horizon. He had to say this now.

"I'm in love with ye, Drew."

13

Tell Me Ye Don't Care

IF CARR BRODERICK had just struck her across the face, Drew would have been less surprised. As it was, she merely stared at him, aware that her lips had parted in shock.

I'm in love with ye.

What was the man saying? Yet he hadn't finished.

"I have been for years," Carr continued, taking a step toward her. "Don't take the veil at Inishail. Come away with me instead."

Drew stared at him, her lips parting. "Carr," she finally managed. "I don't think—"

"Last night meant much to me," he pressed on, his voice raw. Those blue-grey eyes, which she'd once thought so dispassionate, gleamed from the force of the emotions now roiling within him. "It was a claiming. Ye are mine and I am yers."

Drew's mouth clamped shut, and she swallowed. "It was a *coupling*, Carr ... an enjoyable one ... but it can never be more than that."

"Why not?" His gaze narrowed, his throat bobbing.

"I'm a widow about to take the veil, and ye are my guard ... it wouldn't—"

"What does it matter?" he cut in, a nerve flickering in his jaw. "What I feel for ye, transcends everything."

A wave of dizziness swept over Drew. She couldn't believe she was hearing these words. Taciturn, stoic Broderick who'd shadowed her for the past six months, and who'd served her brother loyally for years before that, had just laid his heart bare before her.

"Carr … please don't say such things, I can't—" she began, but he interrupted her once more.

"Why? Because I'm a lowly guard and ye are a high-born lady?"

Drew sucked in a sharp breath. "No, but I … d—don't …," she stuttered, before her voice choked off. Her chest ached and her heart fluttered. Did he really think her so shallow?

"Ye would make a poor nun," he pressed on before she could continue, his face all taut angles now. "Ye can't follow rules … ye will make an enemy of the prioress within days."

Drew gave a sharp laugh. He was likely right, but she wasn't going to admit that. "All my life I've been willful and selfish," she said, recovering her equilibrium. She then folded her arms across her chest. "It's time I learned to follow the rules."

He stepped closer still, the male scent of his skin enveloping her. The sensation of dizziness increased, as did her ache for him. She needed him to move away, she needed some distance between them.

And yet she couldn't move. Her feet felt as if they'd just grown roots.

"Coming away with me wouldn't be selfish," he said softly.

"It would," she replied, stubbornness rising now. "I've already sent word ahead to the priory. Both the prioress and my mother are expecting me."

"Then send word that ye have changed yer mind."

"I can't do that," Drew shot back, frustration rising within her. Why wasn't he listening to her?

"Look me in the eye, and tell me ye feel nothing for me." He ground out the words as he stared deep into her eyes. "Tell me ye don't care … and I will leave ye be."

Drew went still. She really wished he hadn't cornered her like this. She didn't want to be cruel. Why would he make himself so vulnerable before her? He'd just handed her a dirk before baring his chest.

It was as if he wanted her to plunge the knife into his heart.

Reckless fool.

He knew who she was, that she could be ruthless if needed.

Pain lanced through Drew's ears as she clenched her jaw. Her chest started to ache. Suddenly, she hated him for making her do this, for forcing her hand.

She didn't want to part ways with him under a storm cloud, but he'd left her no choice. Why did her life always have to be so hard?

Drew breathed in sharply, her pulse thudding in her ears. Each word hurt her throat, yet she forced them out. "I feel nothing for ye, Broderick."

Carr rode ahead of the company, his gaze scanning the road before him. The sun was shining, basking the pine-clad mountains in unexpected warmth. The wind had died to a brisk breeze that ruffled the horses' manes. Wispy clouds flitted across the sky, and despite that winter was upon them, it seemed as if spring might come early this year.

And yet, Carr paid the sunshine and beautiful surroundings no mind at all. Inside, he felt hollow. His heart was so empty it ached.

He'd taken a great risk—he'd known it the moment he'd demanded the truth from her.

Drew MacKinnon didn't like being pushed into a corner, but he'd done it all the same. He was sick of waiting in the shadows, tired of hiding how he felt.

But the moment he'd said those words, a chill had settled over him.

He'd seen how those expressive grey eyes had shadowed, how her features had tightened. And when she'd told him she felt nothing, that she didn't care from him, it felt as if she'd just punched him in the belly.

At least she didn't lie to ye, he told himself as he urged his courser into a brisk canter up a hill. The breeze whistled against his cheeks, bringing a welcoming sting.

But the thought was no consolation at all, not when it hurt to breathe, hurt to exist.

He'd been wanting to stretch this journey out so that he could savor every last moment he spent with Drew—but now he wished that their destination was in sight. They were making good time, especially while the weather was good. With any luck, they would reach Inishail before dusk the following day.

But that meant he and Drew would still have to spend another evening in each other's company.

A heavy weight settled upon Carr's chest at the thought. He wasn't sure how he was going to endure it.

Drew picked the last piece of meat off the bone—grouse again—and ate it. She had little appetite tonight. Each mouthful was a trial, yet seated at the fire with her escort, she didn't want any of them to fuss over her.

Least of all, Carr Broderick.

Drew swallowed, fighting a wave of nausea before wiping her fingers on the cloth that Aidan passed her.

There was little chance of Carr bothering her. He'd barely glanced her way all day.

Steeling herself, Drew looked across the fire at where he sat, talking to one of the other men. They were discussing the last stretch of the journey. One more day's ride and they'd reach their destination.

At first glance, Carr seemed relaxed this evening, but when she looked closer, Drew saw that wasn't the case. Lines of tension bracketed his mouth and furrowed his forehead. His broad shoulders—shoulders she'd clung to as he'd taken her up against that old oak—were rounded, betraying the unhappiness he hid from the world.

I've hurt him.

The knowledge made Drew feel even queasier. Over the years, after she'd been widowed, she'd spurned the attention of many men. Some had deserved it, and yet there had been one or two who hadn't. Yet she'd barely cared at the time.

She did now.

Tell me ye don't care.

Carr's words from that morning mocked her. He'd now think her a cold, heartless bitch. But the truth of it was that she did care for him. Every time she remembered the hurt in his eyes when she'd rebuffed him, when she'd lied to his face, her belly twisted painfully.

"I think I shall get an early night," she announced to the group, rising to her feet. "Since we have another long day ahead tomorrow."

The rest of the party nodded or smiled, wishing her a good rest. All except Carr. He merely glanced up, his gaze resting upon her for the first time all evening.

And for a moment, they stared at each other.

The raw look in his eyes, the tension in that ruggedly handsome face, made Drew's belly twist once more. The supper she'd eaten churned uneasily in her belly.

I'm sorry. The words whispered through the air between them, unsaid, and yet Drew felt them keenly. She'd never felt sorrier about anything in her life, and yet the stubborn core of resolve within her wouldn't be shifted.

The idea that she'd run away with Carr Broderick—a man who'd served her family for years now—was ridiculous.

Drew tore her gaze from Carr's and stepped away from the fire. She made her way back to her tent, to where someone—most likely Carr—had lit a brazier.

Vision blurring, Drew reached out and warmed her fingers over the low flames.

He's always been so kind to me ... even now.

And yet here she was, reminding herself that a match between them was impossible. They were too different, the gulf between them too wide.

It shouldn't matter and yet it did.

A secret tryst in the dark was one thing, but riding off into the sunset with him was another. The very idea was ridiculous. Carr should realize that too. However, after their night together, he'd been seized by a recklessness that was entirely out of character.

He hadn't been lying. All this time he'd been in love with her, and she'd been too blind to notice.

Drew squeezed her eyes shut. The lump in her throat made it difficult to swallow.

Looking back, she saw it now.

The way his gaze would linger upon her.

How he'd volunteered to become her personal guard and hadn't been unhappy in the slightest that someone else would lead The Dunan Guard.

His loyalty to her, even as she lay in a fever, her body covered in plague boils. He'd barely left her side for days; when the other servants fled the broch for fear of catching the plague, Carr had remained.

And all the while she'd told herself it was because he'd sworn fealty to her family.

But he'd done it for love.

Tears escaped then, trickling down Drew's cheeks. Usually, she hated to weep and would scrub away any treacherous tear. But tonight, she cried silently, her eyes squeezed shut, her chest aching.

14

Beyond Repair

DREW SLEPT BADLY. She passed most of the night staring up at the smoke hole in the tent roof, at a patch of star-strewn sky.

She'd wept at intervals too when the pain in her chest got too much—whenever her thoughts turned to Carr.

Moments from their tryst in the oak woods haunted her. The feel of his mouth on her neck. The way he'd kissed her as if she was a feast he'd been hungering for his whole life.

He was right—it had been a claiming. As she recalled the intensity of their passion, Drew broke out into a cold sweat.

It wasn't the fevered images of their joining that reduced her to tears, but all the kindnesses he'd shown her over the years. Unlike every other man close to her—except for her half-brother, Craeg—he'd never tried to change her. He'd never once implied that she was too aggressive, too mouthy, or too self-centered.

Carr loved her exactly how she was.

And she knew she'd never be accepted by anyone like that again.

An ill mood plagued her when she emerged from her tent. It was a chill, misty dawn. The warmer weather and brighter days had disappeared, and winter's gloom settled over the world once more—almost as if it sensed Drew's dark humor this morning.

Aidan was bent over a small griddle, frying up oatcakes.

"Morning, milady," the young warrior greeted her with a smile. "No butter or honey to go with these I'm afraid ... but they're fresh at least."

Drew favored him with a wan smile and took the two cakes he passed her. They smelled wonderful, yet she had little appetite this morning.

"Thank ye, Aidan," she murmured, before biting into a cake and forcing down a mouthful. As she ate, Drew glanced around. Without even realizing it, she was looking for Carr.

He'd plagued her thoughts all night, had made sleep near to impossible. And when she caught sight of him saddling the horses behind the tents, her chest constricted. Carr had his back to her, yet she could see by the rigidity of his shoulders and back, his jerky movements as he swung a saddle onto a horse's back and did up the girth, that he was unhappy.

She was the cause.

Drew's fingers tightened around the oatcake. If she was a braver person, she'd approach him now and make a proper apology. The man deserved that at least.

I am brave, she reminded herself, setting her jaw. *This needs to be done.*

Leaving the fireside, she circuited the edge of the tents that two men were starting to take down and marched up to Carr.

Hearing someone approach behind him, he turned.

Drew's breathing caught when she saw his face; she was sure she looked pale and strained this morning, but he looked worse.

Dark shadows smudged under his eyes. He almost appeared unwell.

Drew stopped a few feet back from him, aware that she was still clutching her uneaten oatcakes. Holding out the one she hadn't taken a bite from, she smiled. "Here ... I don't imagine ye have eaten yet."

Carr shook his head, his expression stony. "Keep them for yerself, milady ... I shall break my fast when I'm done here."

The cool formality of his tone cut her deeply. Gone was the man who favored her with slow smiles, who'd shared two jugs of wine with her, and who'd spoken of his past. This morning, he was 'Broderick', the aloof guard. He was virtually a stranger.

And yet Drew wasn't that easily put off. Lowering her hand, she kept the weak smile plastered to her face. It was her armor; without it, she'd crumble. "Carr," she began, her voice catching. "I have to say this ... for I might not get a chance later ... I'm sorry. I had no idea ye felt the way ye do. If I had, I wouldn't have asked that favor of ye."

His gaze shadowed, and a chill prickled Drew's skin.

I've just made things worse, she thought dully. *He's angry now.*

"I'm not sorry," he replied roughly. "And I won't be ... ever."

"But this has only hurt ye," she whispered. "I don't want that."

He shook his head. "Leaving ye at Inishail would still have hurt," he said, his voice clipped now. "But this way, ye know how I feel."

The boulder in Drew's belly grew heavier then. "It doesn't change anything, Carr," she whispered, her voice barely audible now. "It just makes our farewell harder ... for us both."

His mouth pinched. He then turned away from her and resumed saddling the horse. "Aye ... it does."

Carr wasn't proud of himself.

He kept his gaze on the buckle he was fastening as he listened to Drew walk away. He'd been cold and harsh—something he never was with her. But her apology—even well-meant as it was—was like a dirk blade to the gut.

Didn't the woman realize? He didn't want her to say sorry, he wanted her to acknowledge that what lay between them was rare and beautiful and that she'd be a fool to turn her back upon it.

Drew MacKinnon wasn't as hard as the world believed. He didn't like how pale and frail she looked this morning. The tremor in her voice made him ache to reach for her. Standing a few feet from Drew and not being able to touch her was torture. Her grey eyes were red-rimmed.

Had she been crying?

He'd never seen the woman he served weep. Surely, he'd been mistaken.

And yet the ache under his breastbone intensified as he let her walk away. She'd wanted to mend things between them. She'd wanted them to be friends again before he dropped her at Inishail Priory, and part of him wanted that too. But the baser part of him wanted to lash out at her.

Dolt, he chided himself. *She told ye she doesn't feel for ye, as ye do for her. Ye must accept it.*

Misery churned in his gut, and for an instant, Carr's eyes flickered shut. He'd always been stoic; he'd always been strong. He'd never been one to fight against fate, or against the hand life had dealt him.

But that was until today.

Despite that Drew had made the nature of their relationship clear the morning before, part of him still fought it.

I can't give up ... I won't give up.

Carr reached up and dragged a hand down his face. It seemed he was intent on wounding his heart beyond repair, on driving that dirk blade in to the hilt.

At the day's end, they'd reach Inishail, and there he'd watch Drew ride through the gates and out of his life forever.

But before she did, he had to try to change her mind—one last time.

The day that followed sped by with frightening speed. Despite the cloak of low cloud that obscured the mountains, and the light veil of rain that settled over everything, the company made excellent time.

This last stretch of the journey to Inishail was upon a surprisingly well-kept road. As noon approached, they forded a river and rode alongside a dark loch framed by lush green mountains wreathed in mist.

Loch Awe. Drew's mother, in her rare missives, had mentioned that the priory sat near the shores of a long, thin loch that stretched for leagues northeast and southwest.

If she hadn't felt so wretched, Drew would have found the landscape pretty; even with the bad weather, she could see that it was a lovely spot. Forest stretched down to the loch-edge in places, and the air was rich with the scent of pine. Two red deer sprinted across the road ahead of them before disappearing like wraiths into the trees.

But Drew could feel nothing except a hard kernel of unhappiness in her gut—a sensation that seemed to grow tighter with every furlong they traveled toward their destination.

They rested briefly at noon, and Drew made sure she avoided looking at Carr. Instead, she forced down cold oatcakes and cheese and listened to the rumble of male conversation around her.

After the morning's humiliation, she couldn't bear to look at him.

She'd tried to apologize, and he'd thrown her words back in her face. Not that she could entirely blame him. As Drew ate her noon meal, she tried not to relive those last few moments.

How bleak his gaze had looked.

They finished their meal quickly and were soon on the road again. Drew rode next to Aidan, while Carr and another took the lead.

"Ye have been quiet today, milady," the warrior observed, and when Drew glanced his way, she saw that the young man was observing her. "Is something amiss?"

Drew inhaled slowly and forced a gentle smile, before shaking her head. She was used to providing a façade to the world; she could do so now too. "The journey has just wearied me, that's all."

"Ye will be looking forward to reaching Inishail then?"

Drew nodded, not trusting herself to speak, lest her voice betray her.

Now that she focused upon it, she was dreading her arrival at the priory—a cold dread that clawed at her belly.

"I'm looking forward to returning to Dunan, milady," the warrior continued, unprompted. Studying his face, she saw the gleam of excitement in his blue eyes. "My love waits for me there."

Drew forced herself to keep breathing steadily, even if an iron band was now tightening around her ribs. "Really ... what's her name?" Her voice was higher than usual, forced, yet Aidan didn't appear to notice.

"Brenna," he replied, grinning widely. "We have been promised to each other for years now ... but as soon as spring arrives, we shall wed. I feel like the most fortunate man alive."

Drew saw the way the young man's face softened as he spoke of his love, how his eyes darkened as he'd said her name.

Swallowing hard, she forced herself to keep smiling, even if her face ached from the effort. However, her next words, when she managed them, were heartfelt. "Brenna is also very fortunate. I wish ye both happiness, Aidan."

15

Parting Ways

INISHAIL PRIORY CAME upon them too soon.

Drew wasn't ready for the sight of the high grey walls, etched against an emerald carpet behind them. As her mother had mentioned, the priory sat near the shores of the loch, less than a furlong back from the pebbly shore. A blanket of milky-white mist crept in from the loch, curling around the base of the priory walls.

And as they approached, an iron bell clanged, tolling through the mist.

Drew tensed. *Vespers.*

From this day forward, her day would be ruled by the clanging of that bell. It would tell her when to rise, when to pray, when to eat, and when to go to bed.

The thought made the queasiness she'd been fighting all day rise in the back of her throat.

The farewells to the men who'd accompanied them were brief, yet Drew held each of their gazes for an instant and wished them a safe return to Dunan.

"Make sure Brenna carries a posy of heather with her when ye wed in the spring," she told Aidan with a conspirator's smile. "It brings good luck."

Her comment made Aidan grin, while around him the other warriors laughed, ribbing the love-struck young man. Only Carr remained still and silent. Waiting while she said her goodbyes to the others. He alone would escort her the last two furlongs to the gate.

Turning her horse, she urged it up next to Carr's, and the pair of them rode in silence up to the arched gateway. When they were a few yards distant, they drew up their horses and dismounted, leading them the rest of the way.

The heavy iron knocker loomed before Drew. That knocker represented safety to so many. A fugitive could claim sanctuary just by touching it, and yet Drew was loath to reach out and curl her fingers around the cold iron.

Instead, she turned to Carr.

He was watching her with that same intense, focused look he'd given her when he'd revealed his feelings.

Please don't gaze upon me like that, she thought, something twisting deep within her chest. His expression made her long to throw herself into his arms, to dig her fingers into his short blond hair, and to ravage his mouth with her own.

But instead, she squared her shoulders and forced herself to remain in the present—to not think about what they'd done together or the things he'd said to her. It was the only way she was going to get through this.

"This is where we part ways," she said softly.

"It doesn't have to be," he replied, stepping close. Suddenly, he was towering above her. "It's not too late. Ye can take my hand now and go. No one but us will know."

Drew stared at him, her pulse thundering in her ears. The Lord give her strength, was he trying to reduce her to a pathetic wreck? It was hard enough as it was to bid him farewell, without him saying these things.

"Yer men will know," she said, her voice hoarse now. "How will ye explain this to them?"

He shook his head, gesturing to where they'd left the others. "They have ridden off, Drew ... there's only me and ye here."

A glance to the left revealed that he'd spoken true. Her escort had gone.

"I won't be returning to Dunan with them," Carr continued, his voice roughening now. "I will travel to the coast and take a boat to Éire, where I will seek out what remains of my kin. I wish for ye to join me ... as my wife."

Drew stared up at him. Her heart was beating so hard that she felt sick. "I've already told ye why I can't do that," she replied, hating the tremor in her voice.

"I don't believe that ye don't care for me," he cut in, a nerve flickering under one eye. "I think ye are lying ... to me and to yerself."

Drew stiffened. "Excuse me?"

"Ye tell me ye must do this ... ye tell me it's because we are too different, that ye have made yer mother a promise, that ye somehow deserve a life of penance." His voice was strained now, each word an effort, and yet he pushed himself on. "But all of it is a weak excuse. The truth, Drew MacKinnon, is that ye are afraid."

Drew's jaw tightened. "I am not."

"Aye, ye are terrified," he countered. "Ye are scared of taking a risk, scared of letting anyone see who ye really are. Ye are afraid of *love*."

His words hung between them, while Drew struggled to breathe. She didn't know what was stronger—the urge to slap his face or to weep.

Before she could do either, Carr continued. "I know ye have been hurt, but ye can trust me, Drew. Ye know that I have only ever cared for ye. I'm offering ye a new life ... I'm offering ye *hope*, and yet ye would throw it all away for certainty. Ye have made yerself a prisoner of yer own fears. If ye do this ... if ye throw this chance away ... ye are nothing more than a coward."

Drew took a shaky step back from him, and then another. A sob welled up in her throat, yet she choked it back. She was crumbling inside, but she couldn't let him see her pain. "Then I am a coward," she whispered.

Carr continued to watch her, his blue-grey eyes narrowing. "I will make camp near the priory ... five furlongs northeast of these walls," he said, his tone harsh with the grief and disappointment that vibrated from him now. "If ye do not come to me by morning, I shall ride away." He paused then, letting his words sink in. "Please don't throw this chance of happiness aside so lightly."

Drew didn't answer. She physically couldn't. Her throat had closed. Her pulse thundered in her ears, and her eyes burned from the urge to cry. But she wouldn't. Not here, not now.

She turned her back on him then. Gathering the last of her self-control, Drew stepped toward the gates. She reached out, her fingers grasping around cold iron, and she knocked.

Coward. Coward. Coward.

With each breath, those words mocked her.

Alone in the prioress's hall, Drew started to pace. As she'd entered the priory during Vespers, she was being made to wait.

The nun who'd met her at the gate hadn't been overly welcoming. She'd cast a jaundiced look at Carr before beckoning Drew inside.

The dull thud of the gate closing behind her had made Drew start to sweat, even as her legs began to tremble. With a huge effort, she'd managed to shove the panic down, and had followed the nun to the stables, where she'd seen to her horse before waiting for the prioress.

Completing another circuit of the narrow hall, her boots whispering upon the flagstones, Drew twisted her fingers together.

Fury now pulsed through her, hot and galvanizing, as she inwardly raged at Carr. *How dare he call me a coward? Who does he think he is?*

And yet, part of her loved that he'd stood up to her. He always had.

But she hadn't been able to look at his face as she'd entered the priory. She hadn't the strength.

The click of a door opening roused Drew from her tormented thoughts. Relieved that she was no longer alone to torture herself, she glanced toward the entrance and saw two women enter.

One was small, with a sharp-featured face that might have once been pretty if sourness hadn't withered it; while the other woman was heavy-set and jowly, a large iron cross resting upon her ample breast.

Drew's gaze immediately went to the first woman. Lorna MacKinnon—now Sister Lorna of Inishail—met her daughter's eye and favored her with a cool smile. "Ye have come sooner than we expected," she greeted her.

Years apart, Ma and that's the best ye can manage?

Her mother had never been the warmest of women, but her years in the priory had made her even colder than Drew remembered.

Drew forced an answering smile. "Aye ... we made good time on the road south."

"I am Mother Iseabal of Inishail," the second woman spoke up. She had a thin, sharp voice that immediately made Drew's irritation rise. "Kneel before me, so I may bless ye."

Drew did as bid, lowering herself on one knee before the prioress, while Mother Iseabal made the sign of the cross above her.

"Ye can rise now," the prioress said, her tone commanding.

Getting to her feet, Drew met the woman's eye and watched the prioress's gaze narrow at her boldness. She obviously wasn't used to others holding her gaze like an equal.

Ye will make an enemy of the prioress within days.

Carr's words came back to her then, and Drew tensed her jaw. Of course the man knew her well; he understood how difficult she'd find it to take orders from anyone, let alone another woman. At the time, Drew had dismissed his comment—he'd been trying to convince her not to take the veil after all.

But now that she stood before the prioress, a chill feathered down her nape.

This woman wasn't like Mother Shona, the former Abbess of Kilbride. Although Drew had never met her, Coira had told her of Mother Shona's warmth, her bravery, and her kindness.

Mother Iseabal dragged a disapproving eye down Drew, taking in her damp clothing and the muddy hems of her kirtle and cloak. "Ye shall enter Inishail as a novice," she informed Drew. "Sister Lorna will take ye to the dormitory so that ye might change into yer habit."

Drew's gaze flicked from the prioress to her mother. Both garbed in black habits and veils, their faces were framed by crisp white wimples.

"What will I do with my clothes?" Drew asked.

"They will be burned," Mother Iseabal replied, her gaze dropping to the rings that Drew wore upon her fingers. "Ye must give me those ... no nun is allowed to wear adornment of any kind."

Drew did as bid, removing the gem-studded gold and silver rings from her fingers and handing them over to the prioress. She'd expected this, yet now that she was about to be admitted into the order, her chest felt tight and sweat trickled between her shoulder blades. How would she feel when she actually donned that crow's garb?

As the prioress took the rings, Drew noted how her fingers tightened possessively over them. Was that an avaricious gleam she'd just seen in the woman's eye?

"I take it, ye shall use the rings to feed the poor, Mother?" Drew asked sweetly. "I'd hate to think that the priory hoards its riches."

"Of course we don't," the prioress snapped, her gaze gleaming with outrage. "We live in poverty here. Go now and change into yer habit. We shall meet again in the kirk for prayers."

16

Ye Have My Heart

"MOTHER ISEABAL SEEMS a ... humorless woman."

Drew's comment broke the uncomfortable hush between mother and daughter as they crossed the yard to the dormitory. It was dark outside now, much later than Drew had thought. They had kept her waiting inside the prioress's hall for longer than she'd realized. Braziers illuminated their path.

Sister Lorna cut her a sharp glance. "She is a god-fearing woman," her mother sniffed. "Which is more than can be said for ye."

Drew arched a brow. "I'm here, aren't I?"

"Aye ... no doubt in penance for the wicked life ye have led."

Drew let her mother's comment lie between them for a few moments, before she answered. "I have flaws, Ma ... but I'm not wicked."

Sister Lorna snorted. "Our Lord will be the judge of that." Her grey eyes narrowed when they focused upon Drew. "Never again address me as yer mother. Here, we are not related ... we are bonded merely in service to God."

Drew held her mother's gaze, unflinching. For years she'd lived in fear of Lorna MacKinnon. When she'd been a bairn, she'd been terrified of her, and of the willow rod she'd used to administer beatings. Their mother had thrashed Duncan the hardest—until he'd grown big and strong enough to fight back—but Drew would never forget the sting of the rod upon her back or the screech of her mother's voice.

An icy sensation settled in the center of Drew's chest as she realized just how much she disliked this woman.

She'd given her life, yet she'd never given her love.

No wonder I'm as I am, Drew thought bitterly. *No wonder I'm afraid of giving my heart to anyone.*

Coward.

Drew's throat thickened then. Aye, Carr was right. But with this woman as her mother, was it any surprise? Part of her had hoped that she'd arrive at Inishial to find her mother changed, that life in the priory might have softened her somehow. But it had not. If anything, it had made her even bitterer.

"Does that *bastard* still rule Dunan?" Her mother said then, her mouth pursing.

Drew inclined her head. "Craeg?"

"Who else do ye think I'd be referring to?"

"Aye ... he's now the MacKinnon clan-chief."

Sister Lorna's face went taut at this admission, and she hurriedly crossed herself. "Ill news, indeed," she muttered. "Yer father would turn in his grave to see such a day."

Drew held her tongue, although she had the urge to point out that Craeg MacKinnon wouldn't exist if it hadn't been for her father's dalliances. Instead, she favored her mother with a wintry smile. "Craeg is an able clan-chief ... a far better one than Duncan ever was. The people love him."

The nun's step faltered at this, her grey eyes turning hard. "How dare ye?" she hissed, and her hand actually raised as if she wished to strike Drew across the face. Drew didn't flinch away. If her mother dared hit her, she'd return the gesture. "Yer brother was the rightful ruler of Dunan," Sister Lorna snarled. "Not this ... this *whoreson.*"

"Duncan made a poor clan-chief ... and don't pretend that ye liked him," Drew countered. "We all knew why ye left. Once Da died, ye were afraid of what Duncan might do ... for ye knew he hated ye. And ye were right, he did."

Sister Lorna's head jerked back as if Drew had indeed just slapped her. She moved back a few paces, her shoulders rounded, her face a mask of fury.

"Ye will learn to curb that viper's tongue here," she hissed, her gaze gleaming with spite. "I have told the prioress of yer wickedness, and she's promised me that she will make ye penitent by the year's end."

With that, Sister Lorna spun on her heel and stalked toward the dark bulk of the dormitories, her spine as stiff as an outraged cat.

Drew watched her go, suddenly rooted to the spot.

Her mother was wrong; she already regretted her sins. She didn't know what had possessed her to throw Duncan's hate in her mother's face. Perhaps she too had a latent need for vengeance, for a chance to get even with this cold, cruel woman.

A sickly sensation rose in Drew's throat. The problem with revenge though, was that the pleasure it brought was short-lived.

I'm turning into her. The thought made her shudder. This was what bitterness did. It poisoned. *In a few years, that will be me.*

Even now, the warmth that Carr Broderick had brought her during this journey, the joy, was starting to fade. Once again, he was right. She was a prisoner of her own fears. For a few short days, she had seen what life could be like if she had the courage to leave the past behind—yet she'd turned her back on it, on him.

Her mother had almost reached the door to the dormitory, and Drew knew that she should go after her, should bend her head and ask forgiveness for her angry words.

But, once again, she couldn't summon the will. It was as if her limbs had turned to stone.

Carr poked the embers with a stick, watching as a spray of sparks shot up into the night. He'd found a dry birch branch for his fire, but it wasn't throwing out much heat. The air was damp and cold tonight—although it was nothing like the chill in his heart.

It felt as if a lump of ice had settled there and would never dislodge.

She's not coming.

Carr didn't want to admit it to himself, and he'd tried to cling onto hope ever since riding away from the priory, but as the night wore on, the truth was becoming clear.

She's not coming, and I'm a fool.

Aye, he was a fool all right, but he'd been a hopeful one. Carr shoved the stick into the embers again, sending more sparks shooting into the heavens. He'd had to take the risk. He'd had to know that all hope was lost.

And now he did.

Muttering a curse, Carr scrubbed a fist over his face. His chest, belly, and head all hurt. He'd ripped himself open before Drew, and he'd been brutally honest with her out there before the gates of the priory.

She probably hates me now.

He couldn't believe how roughly he'd spoken to her. He'd told her she was a coward, for pity's sake. Did he really think that was going to win her over?

If it wasn't the middle of the night, he'd pack up right now and ride away.

She definitely wasn't coming.

Squeezing his eyes shut, Carr leaned his head forward, resting his brow on his clasped hands. His eyelids burned. He hadn't wept in years, but he was on the verge of doing so now. He'd given his heart to a woman who didn't want it; he'd wasted years and years pining after Drew, knowing it was impossible. And yet there had always been a kernel of hope within him.

Until tonight.

How he wished to drown himself in a barrel of ale. The first thing he'd do tomorrow would be to ride to the nearest tavern and drink himself into oblivion.

The pain in his heart couldn't be borne. He needed to escape it; he needed to escape himself.

"Carr!"

A woman's voice cut through his pain, his darkness. He glanced up, blinking as if waking from a dream. Had he been imagining things?

"Carr."

Instinctively, his hand went to his dirk, and he swiveled around to face the figure standing behind him. He'd been so lost in misery, he hadn't even heard her approach. His horse, tethered a few yards away under a tree, snorted nervously.

Before him stood a slight figure, wrapped in a heavy fur mantle. The firelight played across her pale, heart-shaped face and eyes the color of storm clouds.

"Drew," he breathed, stunned. "Ye came?"

A smile curved her lips as she stared down at him. "Aye."

Carr blinked. He'd been so far gone in his despair, he wondered if he'd lost his mind. Maybe he was imagining things. "Is this a dream?"

Her smile widened, her cheeks dimpling. "No ... it's real, Carr."

He leaped to his feet and closed the gap between them in a heartbeat, pulling Drew into his arms. She *was* real—warm and plaint in his arms, her body trembling, her mouth eager under his as he kissed her.

When Carr finally broke off the kiss, they were both gasping for breath. Gazing down at Drew's face, he saw that her cheeks were wet with tears.

"I thought I'd lost ye," he admitted hoarsely, his hands cupping her cheeks as he kissed away her tears. "I imagined it was the end."

"I couldn't do it," she gasped out the words. "Ye were right. I was afraid … terrified in fact."

Leaning down, he kissed her again. This time it was gentle, tender. "*I* was terrified I'd never set eyes on ye again," he murmured against her lips. "Ye have my heart, Drew … ye have for a long time."

Her eyes glittered and tears spilled over once more. He realized then that she was too overcome with emotion to speak.

"What happened?" he whispered. "Did something occur inside the priory … something to make ye change yer mind?"

Her mouth curved at the edges. "Aye … let's say things became clear to me," she murmured, her voice catching. "Things that should have been evident before. Seeing my mother was like having my own future laid out before me. I don't want to become that woman." Drew inhaled a deep, shuddering breath then, trying to regain her shattered composure.

"How did ye get away?" he asked softly. "Surely, they didn't want ye to leave?"

"I didn't ask the prioress's permission if that's what ye mean," she replied, her lips quirking. "I just left." She paused then, her hand rising to his face. There, she traced the lines of his cheek, jaw, and chin with her fingertips, as if committing them to memory. "All these years, Carr, ye have only ever treated me well," she whispered. "Ye have seen the worst of me, and ye still want me. I'd be the most dull-witted woman alive if I turned my back on ye … on us. And if ye will still have me, I am yers."

Carr's breathing caught. Had he heard that right? "Ye are?"

"Aye," she whispered. Her eyes were luminous in the firelight, tears sparkling on her eyelashes. "I love ye, Carr … but I was such a fool that I didn't realize what that actually means." She offered him a watery smile. "Ye have taught me."

Epilogue

I Only Have Eyes for Ye

Belvelly Castle
Cork, Éire (Ireland)

Six months later ...

ROUGH MALE SHOUTS made Drew glance up from her weaving. In the solar, high in the tower keep, she was at work near the chamber's tiny window. Leaving her loom, she peered out, her gaze alighting upon the bailey below.

"What are they doing?" Clara called from behind her.

Drew glanced over her shoulder, her gaze settling upon Clara De La Roche, wife of the man who ruled this castle. Small and red-haired with jade-green eyes, Clara wore an impish expression as she glanced up from her embroidery. "They aren't brawling again, are they?"

"No," Drew replied with an answering grin. "Carr's got them wrestling each other in the dirt."

Clara laughed, cast aside her embroidery, and joined Drew at the window. "This I have to see."

"We're too far away to catch much," Drew replied. However, both women could see that the men had stripped down to their braies, gathered in a semi-circle around two wrestlers locked together.

Clara gave a huff of annoyance. "This won't do." She stepped back from the window and picked up her skirts. "Come ... Drew. Our weaving and embroidery can wait."

With that, Clara turned and hurried from the solar. Still grinning, Drew followed her. They'd been living at Belvelly Castle for over three months now after Carr had taken the position as Captain of The Belvelly Guard. They'd originally gone in search of Carr's kin, only to discover that few of his family now resided in the area. And those who did lived in poverty.

Carr decided to strike out on his own, and shortly after, he'd found this position.

It had taken Drew barely a day to realize that she and Clara would become good friends; the women shared the same wicked sense of humor, the same sharp wit.

Life had been good ever since she and Carr made Belvelly their home. As soon as they'd gotten settled, Drew sent word to Dunan. She'd known that Craeg and Coira would be worrying about her. In her missive, she let them know she was safe and well—and living in Éire with Carr Broderick.

The women descended the narrow stone steps, wending their way to the bottom of the tower keep and into the Great Hall that made up most of that level. The noon meal approached, and the servants were busy setting the long tables that lined the chamber. The aroma of mutton stew and baking bread wafted through the keep.

Outdoors in the bailey, the wrestling continued. And as she approached the group of warriors, Drew realized that one of the wrestlers was her husband.

Husband. She got a warm glow in the pit of her belly whenever she thought of Carr that way. It was ridiculous really, for they'd been wed nearly six moons now, yet she still felt as giddy as a blushing sixteen-year-old maid around him.

Her gaze feasted upon him now, naked to the waist. His muscular torso gleamed with sweat. Years ago, Drew had thought of Carr as 'stocky', yet the first time she'd seen him naked, she'd realized there wasn't any fat on him. His body was pure muscle.

"This is entertaining, is it not?" Clara whispered to Drew, linking arms with her. "I must say, yer husband is a fine specimen."

Drew smiled, although she never took her gaze off Carr. As they watched, he hooked his leg through his opponent's and brought him crashing to the ground. The onlookers cheered and clapped, as did Drew and Clara.

Breathing hard, Carr straightened up. He wiped the sweat off his brow and exchanged a few words with the man next to him before he realized they had a female audience. His gaze widened. "Drew ... Lady Clara. This is hardly a place for ladies."

Clara gave a delicate snort. "I must ask ye to practice wrestling with Conor sometime ... now that's a sight I'd enjoy."

This comment brought guffaws of laughter from the surrounding warriors. Conor De La Roche, Baron of Belvelly, was a huge bull of a man. One that few would want to wrestle with.

However, Carr grinned at this. The sight made Drew's heart flutter. It was so good to see him smile. It made Drew realize how much happier he was these days. Dunan had cast a shadow over him as much as it did her.

Here in Éire, they were both lighter, freer, as if a heavy mantle had been lifted from their shoulders.

Taking a drying cloth that one of his men handed him, Carr approached Drew. Perhaps realizing she was intruding, Clara moved away to talk to one of the guards, giving them a few moments alone.

"I enjoyed that," Drew greeted him with a pert grin. "I hadn't realized how much I love watching half-naked men fight."

Carr smiled, a slow, sultry expression that made her belly melt like hot tallow. "I aim to please, wife," he said softly, before bowing his head to kiss her. Oblivious to the fact that they stood in the midst of the bailey, surrounded by men and horses, he deepened the kiss.

Drew stood on tip-toe, her lips parting under his. Pulling back, she realized her pulse was racing. "The noon meal is almost ready," she murmured, breathless now. "Will ye come inside with me?"

He nodded. "Just let me get my léine." He turned and retrieved his tunic from one of the guards. He then pulled it over his head and took Drew by the hand, leading her back toward the keep.

"I'm not sure I want ye coming out here to watch me wrestle," he said with a wink. "The other warriors stare too much at my pretty wife for my liking."

Drew laughed, the sound carrying over the bailey as she squeezed his hand. "Let them stare. I only have eyes for ye."

She meant it too. The connection she and Carr shared was powerful and grew stronger with each passing moon. She'd almost lost him once, through her own blindness, and she'd never let that happen again.

Carr smiled down at her, his gaze soft now. He drew her hand up, placing it over his heart, letting her feel its strong, steady beat. "And I for ye, mo chridhe," he whispered.

The End

From the author

Some stories just have to be written! I don't know about you, but Drew and Carr intrigued me right from Book #1. During the first draft of UNFORGOTTEN, I realized that I wanted to tell their story ... I just wasn't sure in what format. It wasn't going to be a full-length novel, and it certainly merited more than a short-story.

So instead, it ended up being a kind of 'epilogue novella' for THE SISTERS OF KILBRIDE series. At 30,000 words, I'd like to think I have done their romance justice.

Characters like Drew and Carr are so easy to write about. She's feisty and willful, a woman that would scare many men off. But Carr sees past all that. I must admit, I'm a sucker for 'unrequited love' stories. I love writing about the longing, the frustration, and then the moment the balance of power between the two characters starts to shift. CLAIMED ended up being more angsty and sexy than I'd anticipated. As always, writing a romance between two more 'mature' characters, especially where the heroine is a few years older than the hero, gives me more scope during sex scenes. This wasn't a story about a blushing virgin!

I hope you found CLAIMED as fun to read as I did to write. Sadly, we now come to the end of THE SISTERS OF KILBRIDE. But fear not, dear reader, I have plenty more stories in store for you!

Jayne x

About the Author

Award-winning author Jayne Castel writes epic Historical and Fantasy Romance. Her vibrant characters, richly researched historical settings, and action-packed adventure romance transport readers to forgotten times and imaginary worlds.

Jayne has published a number of bestselling series. In love with all things Scottish, Jayne also writes romances set in Dark Ages Scotland … sexy Pict warriors anyone?

When she's not writing, Jayne is reading (and re-reading) her favorite authors, cooking Italian feasts, and going for long walks with her husband. She lives in New Zealand's beautiful South Island.

Connect with Jayne online:
www.jaynecastel.com
www.facebook.com/JayneCastelRomance/
https://www.instagram.com/jaynecastelauthor/
Email: contact@jaynecastel.com

* 9 7 8 0 4 7 3 5 4 7 5 8 5 *